PERFECTION

Vincenzo Latronico was born in Rome in 1984 and currently lives in Milan. He has translated many books into Italian, by authors such as George Orwell, Oscar Wilde, F. Scott Fitzgerald and Hanif Kureishi. *Perfection* is his fourth novel, the first to be translated into English.

Sophie Hughes is a translator of Spanish and Italian literature. Her translation of Alia Trabucco Zerán's *The Remainder* was shortlisted for the International Booker Prize, as was her translation of Fernanda Melchor's *Hurricane Season*. Her work has appeared in the *Guardian*, the *Paris Review*, *The White Review*, *frieze* and the *New York Times*. She lives in Italy.

'*Perfection* is a jewel of a novel: precisely cut, intricately faceted, prismatically dazzling at its heart. Vincenzo Latronico is the finest of writers.'
— Lauren Groff, author of *The Vaster Wilds*

'Vincenzo Latronico is a writer who sees clearly and conveys it beautifully. I can't recommend *Perfection* highly enough.'
— Lauren Oyler, author of *Fake Accounts*

'This book gives startling form to the question of how to live a meaningful life; to the illusion that appearance is beauty; to the restlessness of contemporary society. I read it in a breath and I was captivated.'
— Ayşegül Savaş, author of *The Anthropologists*

'Never has a novel so incisively captured what it feels like to participate in the globalized culture of the internet era: to consume it; to be overwhelmed by it; to try, futilely, to make it. *Perfection* is satire in the way that adult life itself is a comedy. By its end, the novel will cure you of any dream for authenticity.'
— Kyle Chayka, author of *The Longing for Less*

'Sharp and revelatory. Latronico is a brilliant and fearless writer. I recommend this novel to every reader I meet.'
— Ellena Savage, author of *Blueberries*

'An important novel, innovative in its own way.'
— Claudia Durastanti, author of *Strangers I Know*

'*Perfection* is a generation-defining piece of literature, one that spares us nothing. To read it is to look in a mirror and finally, for the first time, truly see yourself and the culture you've helped create: the one that lurks behind the filters, algorithms and curated ephemera of selfhood that make up our public lives. Read it and tremble.'
— Madeleine Watts, author of *Elegy, Southwest*

'The world of this horrifying novel has been built piece by perfect piece – honey-colored floorboards, a monstera's perforate leaves, glossy white tiles, a breakfast of assorted seeds, a game of Carcassonne – the method of its construction likewise perfect, a perfection of prose that ends by releasing, miraculously, the very thing perfection is made to prohibit, the heavy stink of mortality.'
—— Kathryn Davis, author of *Aurelia, Aurélia*

'The book artfully lays out detail upon detail of Anna and Tom's quotidian existence in forensic, deadpan style.... But where is reality, Latronico asks in this sharp, deliciously pessimistic novel.... [A]lienation from the self is at the hollow, restless heart of Anna and Tom's lives: constantly yearning, empty of meaning. Latronico's thought-provoking book is anything but.'
—— Thomas McMullan, *Guardian*

'*Perfection* is a short, sly, scathing satire about dissatisfied millennials.... But [it] offers something more than amusing social stereotypes. It is a devastating critique of aspirational consumerism and personal branding, of a generation's "identical struggle for a different life", in a world where the principal means of expressing their agency is through food and fonts.... Latronico's piercing irony is translated with great care and dexterity by Sophie Hughes, meaning it all feels painfully familiar.... Latronico has written one of the most brilliantly controlled works of social realism I've read in a while.'
—— Johanna Thomas-Corr, *Sunday Times*

'*Perfection* is a defining picture of a generation.... [A] curious and compelling read – like staring into a mirror for the first time, unsure whether to be struck by wonder or terror. Whichever it was, I couldn't look away.'
—— Chris Allnutt, *Financial Times*

'*Perfection* captures with uncanny precision the sorry state of things in an era where abundance – of choices, of possessions, of personal freedoms – has brought the opposite of fulfilment.'
— Sarah Moorhouse, *Spectator*

'I breathed in *Perfection* by Vincenzo Latronico, a short but vivid novel about a restless millennial couple living in Berlin, which is hitting shelves mid-February. With its characters' withering ambitions, forest of houseplants and WFH-induced cabin fever, I think the young Italian author has done well to capture the spirit of the 2020s.'
— Ceci Browning, *The Times*

'*Perfection* gave me the gift of being able to hold a long span of time – in a relationship, in a city – and the experience of being young, and the experience of being not so young – all in my head at once. I could hold it there the way you hold a parable or fable, but with all these tiny details, too. It also functioned like a kind of murder mystery: what slowly killed the magic? Was it their values, was it aging, was it... was it...? It's such a beautiful, thoughtful, impeccably crafted book.'
— Sheila Heti, author of *Pure Colour*

'I read *Perfection* in a single hypnotized sitting. Time disappeared, as it does for Anna and Tom. In the following days, I described the book to myself with words like "flat" and "clinical" and "affectless". I thought of it as a "case study" or a "kind of ethnography". Reading it again a week later, I had the impression of meeting a beautiful, well-dressed person for the second time and realising only then, with some embarrassment, that they were smart and funny and sensitive. *Perfection* is dense with ideas, feelings, political insights, beautiful turns of phrase, unexpected observations about ordinary occurrences – all the qualities I look for (and appreciate in real time) when reading fiction.'
— Alice Gregory, *New Yorker*

Fitzcarraldo Editions

PERFECTION

VINCENZO LATRONICO

Translated by

SOPHIE HUGHES

For Alma

'That was where real life was, the life they wanted to know, that they wanted to lead.'
—— Georges Perec, *Things: A Story of the Sixties*, tr. David Bellos

PRESENT

Sunlight floods the room from the bay window, reflects off the wide, honey-coloured floorboards and casts an emerald glow over the perforate leaves of a monstera shaped like a cloud. Its stems brush the back of a Scandinavian armchair, an open magazine left face-down on the seat. The red of that magazine cover, the plant's brilliant green, the petrol blue of the upholstery and the pale ochre floor stand out against the white walls, their chalky tone picked up again in the pale rug that just creeps into the frame.

The next picture is of the building's exterior, an Art Nouveau apartment block with acanthus leaf and citrus fruit cornices. The white render is all but invisible under layers of fluorescent graffiti, tattered posters and peeling paint. On the first floor, you can scarcely make out the stucco tympanums beneath the grime. The combination of turn-of-the-century luxury and raw modern grittiness lends a feeling of freedom and decadence, with a hint of eroticism. Some of the windows are boarded up with faded chipboard, but in others there are plants and string lights. An ivy cascades from a balcony onto the street below.

The kitchen is fitted out with glossy white subway tiles, a chunky wooden worktop, a double butler's sink. Open shelves are lined with blue and white enamel dishes and mason jars filled with rice, grains, coffee, spices. Cast-iron pans and olive wood ladles hang from a wall-mounted steel bar. Out on display on the worktop are a brushed steel kettle, a Japanese teapot and a bright red blender. The windowsill is filled with herbs growing in terracotta pots: basil, mint, chives, but also marjoram, winter savory, coriander, dill. Pushed against one wall is an antique marble-top pastry table and salvaged school

13

chairs. They are lit by an accordion wall-light mounted between a botanical lithograph of an araucaria and a reproduction print of a British wartime poster.

Next, the living room, where a jungle of low-maintenance, luxuriant plants shelter in the nook of the bay window: the lush monstera stretching its shiny leaves towards the outside world, a fiddle-leaf fig almost touching the ceiling from its huge faux-concrete pot, trailing ivies and hanging peperomia on display across two wall shelves, and string of pearls and Chinese money plants whose tangled foliage reaches all the way to the floor. In one corner, arranged on a collection of stools and upturned boxes, is a miniature forest of alocasias, giant euphorbias, weeping figs, downy-stemmed philodendrons, strelitzias and dieffenbachias. Through the French window you can make out a balcony with two chairs around a small table, a porcelain ashtray and some string lights.

The reverse perspective shows the rest of the room: a low sofa and Danish curved mahogany armchair upholstered in petrol-blue textured cotton; a herringbone tweed blanket; an exposed lightbulb with a twiddly filament hanging from a midnight-blue fabric cable; a black metal side table with past issues of *Monocle* and the *New Yorker* stacked beside a brass candle holder and a glass bowl filled with fruit. Next, a rolltop wooden sideboard displaying spider plant cuttings in glass jars of water, an avocado seed just starting to sprout, and a vinyl record player; two floor-standing speakers connected to an amplifier on a low wall shelf; above that, an LP collection with a few prized pieces facing outwards (a limited edition *In Rainbows*, a first edition Kraftwerk); a dracaena casting a shadow like a spindly hand; a Primavera Sound poster.

Tying it all together is a sandy-coloured Berber rug

14

with a fine geometric pattern. On either side of the room there are facing double doors, stripped but with the odd streak of pistachio paint still visible. The doors are closed, which gives the modest space a cosy, intimate, almost cramped feel. It is a room for low-lit, hushed conversations on winter evenings. But in the next picture, those same four doors, now wide open, offer a view of the connecting rooms, and the perspective is lengthened again by the line of the hardwood floorboards.

The room on the left is a home office set up for two. Inside it, a large, white melamine blockboard desk with hairpin legs is arranged as facing workstations: each holds a monitor, a wireless keyboard, an Anglepoise lamp and a pair of over-ear headphones in garish colours. One of the workstations has a seventies swivel chair with a moulded plywood seat, the other a wooden ergonomic kneeling chair with black upholstery. The back wall has floor-to-ceiling shelves lined with paperbacks and graphic novels, most in English, interspersed with illustrated coffee table books – monographs on Noorda and Warhol, Tufte's series on infographics, the Taschen history of typefaces, and another Taschen on the entryways of Milan. In place of bookends there are succulents in cement plant pots, a waist-level camera, a few boardgames – Scrabble, Risk, Catan. Over in one corner you can make out a router and an A3 printer.

There is only one picture of the bathroom, which has a single slit window but is nonetheless bright, thanks to all the reflective surfaces. A lush trailing ivy drapes itself across the window from the curtain pole, picking out the dazzling green of the mosaic floor tiles, which also run up the side of the inset bath. On a cylindrical cabinet with sliding doors the eye is drawn along a skyline of little bottles and vials, all by different brands but with similar

15

labels in white, pink or light grey, the names printed in lightweight sans-serif fonts.

On the opposite side of the living room there is a bedroom with an extra-deep double mattress resting on a tatami base. The headboard is hidden from view by four oversize pillows, and the duvet is spread with a vintage quilt, the only splash of colour among the creamy bedlinen, white walls and pale yellow tatami. There are two reading lights, one on either side of the bed – slim metal cylinders with more decorative bulbs; two symmetrical clothes stands on either side of an antique travel trunk; a yoga mat rolled up in one corner beside some dumbbells and a resistance band. All the pictures are brightly lit and in focus but one: it's of the same bedroom but now in semi-darkness, the curtains drawn, the walls streaked with that orangey light that filters into a room when you wake up late and the sun is already high, and maybe it's a Sunday, or maybe it's not.

The life promised by these images is clear and purposeful, uncomplicated.

It is a life of coffees taken out on the east-facing balcony in the spring and summer while scrolling *New York Times* headlines and social media on a tablet. The plants are watered as part of a daily routine that also includes yoga and a breakfast featuring an assortment of seeds. There is work to be done at a laptop, of course, but at a pace more befitting an artist than an office worker: between intense bursts of concentration at a desk there might be a walk, a videocall with a friend who has an idea for a new project, some jokes exchanged on social media, a quick trip to the nearby farmers' market. They are long days – altogether, the working hours probably exceed those of an office worker – and yet, unlike in an office, here no one is counting hours, because in this life work plays an important role without being an obligation or burden. On the contrary, work is a source of growth and creative stimulation, the bassline to the tune of leisure.

But it is also a life with room for joy, which is clear from every little detail. The long days are followed by a mandatory hour offline to go out for a drink or flick through a magazine while curled up on the sofa, shielded from the cold. Beauty and pleasure seem as inextricable from daily life as particles suspended in a liquid.

And it is a happy life, or so it seems from the pictures in the post advertising the apartment for short-term rental at one hundred and eighteen euros a day, plus the fee to cover the Ukrainian cleaner, paid through a French gig economy company that files its taxes in Ireland; plus the commission for the online hosting platform, with offices in California but tax-registered in the Netherlands; plus another cut for the online payments system, which has its headquarters in Seattle but runs its European subsidiary out of Luxembourg; plus the city tax imposed by Berlin.

IMPERFECT

Reality didn't always live up to the pictures.

In the mornings it often would. Waking up, the sight of filtered light dancing on the walls would instantly put them in a good mood. Yesterday's clothes would be strewn over the clothes stands. Their phones, having charged overnight, would be glaring rectangles on the dusty covers of two open books with their spines facing up. They would check their emails and social media from bed, their faces blue from the backlit screens, looking like a young professional couple in Berlin, which is exactly what they were.

But the moment they set foot in the living room, that confidence would start to falter, like a previously clear voice on a phone losing signal.

The plants would be permanently caked in a thick layer of dust, which polish only seemed to attract more quickly. Streams of direct sunlight would fall on the floating dust motes, giving the impression the apartment had been shut up for years, but in winter it would be too cold to air it out because the windows were old and the radiators too small to keep the space heated. Only rarely did they muster the patience and resolve to clean the double-paned windows, which were covered in tiny constellations of milky smudges that would appear brighter as spring turned to summer.

Desk-sharing didn't suit them. He preferred working from the sofa, and her mugs, Post-its and pens had a habit of migrating to his side of the desk, where, to save time, they would also often eat lunch, leaving greasy stains on the white melamine. The dishwasher was too big for two people's dishes so they had bought a plastic dish rack which took up most of the worktop. An old towel had been placed underneath it to protect the wood from even more water damage.

And then there were the things. Things absolutely everywhere: the chargers, the receipts, the bicycle pump, and the endless stream of forms and reminders that constituted German bureaucracy; the herpes cream, the tissues – fresh packs, used, or scraps that had been through the wash – the felt wool insoles, the sunglasses case, the odd glove they still hoped to match with its pair, the tangled earphones. Moving from room to room, their vision still hazy from sleep, they would take it all in at a glance, each new item on the list adding to a feeling of physical discomfort that was more than irritation – it bordered on distress.

Over the course of the day, more out-of-place objects and signs of slovenliness would enter their field of vision, breaking their concentration. They would come off a call or look up from a difficult email and see themselves from the outside, surrounded by leftover takeaways and scraps of paper, a bathrobe flung over the Danish armchair, and they would feel flawed, like impostors in a grown-up world that would have caught them out already had the webcam lens been any wider.

It wasn't order they so desperately craved, but something deeper and more essential. They lived in a country whose language they didn't speak, in a job with unclear boundaries and no fixed hours or base, and which was, to a great extent, subject to the whims of their clients and social media contacts. The environment where they slept and worked, and which they themselves had chosen and shaped, was the one tangible manifestation of who they were. That apartment and those objects weren't merely reflections of their personalities: they provided a foothold, in their eyes proof of a grounded lifestyle, which, from another perspective (that of, say, their parents' generation) appeared loose. In itself, chaos could be joyful, creative; but in that context, it only seemed to signal impermanence.

These ideas weren't at the forefront of their minds every time they went to tidy up, but they did provide the background music when, each morning, they would painstakingly restore the apartment to its factory settings. Waiting for the coffee to brew, they would switch on the lamps in each corner of the room, plump the sofa cushions, fold the herringbone blanket, remove any mouldy fruit from the bottom of the large glass bowl and wash the mugs, or else shove them in the dishwasher. By the time they sat down for breakfast, all would be as it should be, and for ten unspoiled minutes they would sip their coffee, scrolling through their social media and newsfeeds, ready to start the day.

All that resplendent order would have begun to crumble by lunchtime under the strain of countless mundane tasks (the mail, their head cold, that urgent phone call), almost as if reality were fighting back to reassert its superiority.

Two or three times a year they would put more energy into their interventions. On those occasions – whenever they flew home to their southern European city for the holidays, or to escape the harsh northern winters – they would sublet the apartment for what was, even to them, an extortionate price. It was usually rented by tourists looking for an authentic experience of the city, many of them visiting from Anna and Tom's own country. In addition to the house keys, on arrival they would receive a note both friendly and exuding *savoir vivre*, listing farmers' markets and neighbourhood dining spots. Other times, though, it would be new arrivals to the city needing a base while they searched for more permanent accommodation. Dealing with these guests never failed to remind them that they had made the right choice: in their email exchanges, Anna and Tom would warn the newcomers that prices in the city had risen sharply. If it was a permanent lease they wanted, they would need a decent level of German to wade through the complicated paperwork. Anna and Tom would put them in touch with online expat communities and occasionally invite them out for drinks, once they had found their own place. Some of them would end up joining their circle of friends – if they settled, if they survived the string of short-term sublets and their first winter.

Whatever the reason for their stay, it was crucial those guests got what they paid such a premium for: Anna and Tom's earning potential hinged on their satisfaction. And so, before leaving Berlin, they would devote several hours to taming reality to make it fit the images they had sold.

The bulk of these clean-up operations usually happened in the evenings because they tended to travel on the cheap, early morning flights. Having finished work for the day, they would pack their bags, then set about stuffing every last trace of reality into huge, clear storage boxes, which they then stacked one on top of the other in the attic. In would go the invoices and shoes, the beauty products, the mismatched plates they ate from (leaving the blue and white enamel ones for the guests). They would line up the glasses on the open shelves in the kitchen, clear their paperwork from the table, stock up the fruit bowl and refill the matching candleholders. Next, they would line up the barely opened magazines in the rack, stash their food in the cupboard, return the books left lying around to their shelves, and throw all their worn-but-not-dirty clothes to the back of the wardrobe. After that they would print off the house instructions – wifi password included – and leave them and the welcome pack – lemons and fresh ginger, coffee, Club-Mate, Sekt – on the kitchen worktop. Finally, they would pre-fill the coffee maker to save time in the morning before leaving, which by that point would be in just four or five hours' time.

Waking up in the dark, they would turn on all the lights, hastily change the sheets and dump the dirty bedding and damp towels in the bathroom cabinet, then wash up their still warm espresso cups. With the boxes in the attic and their suitcases on the landing, they would do one last round of the place to make sure everything was in order before locking up. They would survey each room in silence: all those clear surfaces, all that free space, everything finally in its place in the violet light of dawn. For a few glorious seconds they would see their apartment just as they wanted it, perfectly superimposable onto the pictures.

Finally, they would dash to catch the airport bus, dark circles under their eyes and their suitcases clattering along the rutted streets of Neukölln.

Anna and Tom were creative professionals, a term even they found vague and jarring. Their exact titles varied depending on the job, but they were always in English, even in their native language: web developer, graphic designer, online brand strategist. What they created were differences.

They hadn't actively chosen that line of work. It had formed out of their passions, more or less at the same time the internet – their teenage obsession – had crystallized into an industry destined to subsume all others. They had got into music just as online piracy was prompting the rise of peer-to-peer networks. At the end of the school day, their long afternoons would be spent jumping between History and Maths homework and Photoshop and Flash, feeling their way blindly through bugs and mistakes as they tried to improve their GeoCities sites. They would spend hours building personal websites and profiles that reflected their tastes and interests, lists of things that made them special.

This passion of theirs wasn't learned. It was a natural consequence of the context in which they had grown up.

The web was chaotic and surprising, its elusive resources the stuff of legend. Social media didn't exist yet and indexing was done manually: an interesting web page or a repository of hacks or pre-Napster music were prized discoveries, a sign of good taste and expertise. Anna and Tom would fill whole pages with them, use sprites and animated GIFs to embellish them, constantly update links to new pages, and embed visitor counters and animated drop-down menus using JavaScript. If a design feature caught their eye, they would download the code and add a version of it to their site.

The internet came of age with them. Like their own entrance into adulthood, it didn't happen overnight, but gradually, in a way that only seemed inevitable after the fact. There must have been a precise moment when knowing their way around Dreamweaver no longer constituted a hobby but a professional qualification, just as there must have been a first time they logged on to a website using their real names as opposed to some vaguely Anglo-American-sounding pseudonyms. They had started paying social security contributions the same year in which – after a long and painful wait – they were finally able to join Facebook.

Ever since Anna and Tom first started using computers, there was always someone calling in a favour: to format a hard drive, to work on the school newspaper homepage or a friend of the family's jewellery website or their study group wiki. Slowly but surely, the favours turned into paid gigs – an uncle's e-commerce site, business cards, posters, banners, menus – and before long that assortment of odd jobs had coalesced into a real job.

And a sought-after job at that. Anna and Tom had grown up with the notion that individuality manifested itself as a set of visual differences, immediately decodable and in constant need of updating. They were well prepared by the time the demand to express what makes each person *special* had spread from teenage online profile pages to brands, companies, shops and professionals all over the world. Everyone wanted a website, logo or graphic. Everyone sought a little beauty, a unique point within a coordinate system of differences. Anna and Tom understood this need instinctively.

In a way, it was also the reason they had moved to Berlin. After graduating and starting out in their careers, life in a large but peripheral southern European city soon started to feel dull, tedious. It seemed to run on a fixed set of tracks: the same old neighbourhoods, the same summer spots, the same friends they'd had since school. The music scene, the décor in the restaurants and bars, and even their clients' tastes had something provincial and outdated about them. The cliques were hotbeds of gossip; conformist attitudes fostered what Anna and Tom felt to be stifling expectations. And among those people – who never changed, who were content to hang out in the same sets they belonged to at school – Anna and Tom weren't free to be themselves, or rather, they weren't free to reinvent themselves.

Of course, just as the visual points of difference they sold to their clients were also sold to thousands of others by creative professionals all over the western world, an identical struggle for a different life motivated an entire sector of their generation. And yet this knowledge registered only in the vaguest sense. Viewed from the inside, that trend took on the appearance of mythology: their decision to move abroad, made on a whim in a bar at a time when work was getting them down but their savings were high. The airport at dawn with three huge suitcases and ski jackets for the winter (they even took a picture of themselves in the reflection of the terminal doors, padded out in the double layer of jumpers they had put on to avoid the excess baggage fee). The initial string of short-term flat shares in Friedrichshain. The Kreuzberg studios used as crash pads. The sofa beds in Neukölln. The vast, empty apartments with honey-coloured floorboards and monsteras shaped like clouds. The afternoon beers on the dusty banks of the Landwehrkanal or in the illogically treeless Tempelhof Park. The days spent working from the cafés dotted along Rosenthaler Straße like rosary beads. The first winter, that piercing, unimaginable cold which would bring tears to their eyes as they waited for the M29, and made the bottles they left chilling in the snow on the balcony explode in a matter of minutes. The open-end lease for the two-bed apartment in Reuterkiez secured by forging an employment contract they found online. The Google Translate German patchily memorized whenever they were confronted with the city's realities: Kurzstrecke. Krankenkasse. Rohrreinigungsspirale. Vorderhaus. Steuernummer. Ich hätte gerne. Steuer-ID. Schlüsseldienst. An die Ecke. Schwangerschaftsverhütungsmittel. Vielleicht. Ebenso. The warehouse parties. The house parties at Jugendstil apartments in Prenzlauer Berg with bay windows and period mouldings. Berghain. The gallery parties. The barge parties on the Spree. The blurry journeys home on the U-Bahn, which ran all night. Visionäre. Renate. The illegal parties in Wedding sought but never found, when they would wander from one abandoned warehouse to the next, clinging to an SMS message containing directions. Rodeo. Tresor. The blood-red light of northern sunsets. The pearly white dawn bursting unexpectedly through the huge glass walls at Panorama Bar, but which everyone there knew was an illusion, because on the other side of that dawn, the night would go on.

When they weren't busy moving apartments, Anna and Tom spent much of their first year in Berlin carefully constructing this mythology. And it wasn't personal to them; its value lay precisely in its universality. It was a mythology shared by all the Spaniards, French, Italians and Americans they met. It was the topic of countless lifestyle articles and documentaries, and circulated on the Facebook timelines and Instagram feeds of an entire generation. It was the admission stamp into a community bound by a shared reality, or quasi-reality.

Unlike their old life, that reality was characterized by abundance, chiefly of time: with everything being so

27

cheap, there was no need to work long hours, which left them time for other things. They had held on to a couple of clients who provided enough work typesetting reports and B2B publications to guarantee them a minimum income. They grew their client portfolio via word of mouth or friends who couldn't take on any more work. They made good money, compared to their university friends from home. Or bad money, compared to the people who did the same work but for German clients. Not that they knew anyone who did. The few commissions they took on that were actually based in Berlin – the microbreweries and vegan bakeries, the tour companies and co-working spaces – came exclusively from within their own circles.

They designed grids for product catalogues, developed CSS frameworks for e-commerce sites, personalized WordPress themes. Their style was simple, intimate, in keeping with an aesthetic that was starting to be seen all over the world, from the landing pages of start-ups in Stockholm, to restaurant menus in Brooklyn, to the feature pages of London-based fashion magazines: grids with wide, asymmetrical margins; teal green and dusty pink; slightly rounded corners; lightweight Swiss fonts with tight kerning; microinteractions. They were basic tricks, but the resulting visual balance gave off a casual coolness mostly inaccessible to the graphic designers back home. In Berlin that style radiated from every gourmet burger joint and concert poster. Anna and Tom breathed it in. They felt like conduits for that breath of cosmopolitan air into provincial Europe. That was another reason it made sense for them to be there.

The job required patience and precision, and a particular kind of concentration compatible with the bustle and background music of cafés. It also demanded creativity, mostly in the form of making tiny tweaks to existing

28

frameworks. Did they like the job? Yes, but they would reformulate the question. They did for money now what they used to do out of passion. This was a fact. From this fact they concluded that they had turned their passion into a job. This was a deduction.

Nonetheless, that deduction was largely confirmed by how time would disappear whenever they really got their heads down to work on a layout or wireframe. They would listen to LCD Soundsystem and Animal Collective on repeat on their headphones, tweaking a grid, checking paragraph styles, perfecting all the variations of a colour scheme, and before they knew it the morning would have disappeared – or a whole week, or an entire winter. It was the opposite of boredom, when time seems to stand still – which had to mean it was fun.

The time that did not disappear through work was taken up by the city. Berlin was, to all intents and purposes, their main pastime – exploring it, understanding it, feeling part of it. In a way it defined them much more than their profession did. They liked their work but not enough to give more to it than was absolutely necessary. They had fallen into the job. Berlin, on the other hand, they had chosen.

They would go for walks on endless summer evenings and freezing winter mornings when the blinding sunlight would reflect off the fresh snow. They would gaze up in awe at the vast and changeable northern sky, so different from the one under which they had grown. They could spend hours roaming the narrow cobbled streets of Schillerkiez, or the linden-lined squares of the grander end of Mitte, marvelling at every little detail: the jungles of tropical plants behind the windows, the geometric pattern of the flagstone pavements. They were fascinated by the contrast between the recently renovated buildings and those still bearing the shabbiness of the former East – the crumbling or graffitied stucco, the boarded-up windows. They were envious of the legendary period in the nineties when everything had been up for grabs and apartments the length of an entire block could be squatted or else rented for a pittance. There wasn't just an abundance of time in Berlin, but also of space.

Of course, it was history that had hollowed out that space. Anna and Tom understood this, or at least they would have if they had ever thought it through. They could make vague connections between place names and crucial events from the previous century, and naturally they were aware of the Wall and the broken glass, but really their awareness didn't exceed a few anecdotes rattled off to make it look like their life there had more substance. It never occurred to them, for example, that the distinction between Alt- and Neu- buildings in property listings had been drawn by the Allied bombings. Whenever a guest asked them for a tour of the city, Anna and Tom would come out with the same anecdotes – about punk rock gigs in church basements, refugees climbing the Wall, the 'Candy Bomber' – polishing them through repetition until they bore a faint resemblance to a story from one of their parties.

This lack of awareness was reflected in their limited knowledge of the city's topography. They knew where the most touristy sections of the Wall were, but they had never tried to work out its full course. In their minds they mostly hung out in former East Berlin, because that was what they associated with the derelict apartment blocks and the feeling of abundance and freedom. But to them East Berlin included Kreuzberg and Neukölln – actually in the former West – and not Pankow and Marzahn, where 'East' really just meant rows and rows of Soviet housing estates, and where they never had any reason to go. Wedding, in the west, existed only very faintly on their mental map, even though with every year it seemed to take on more substance, as if slowly coming into focus. They only ever ventured to Charlottenburg to buy champagne for New Year's Eve.

The collective upheaval of the twentieth century was over and the vestiges had been translated into the language of individualism – that is, of consumerism. Freedom had turned into abundance. Undeveloped lots and deserted housing blocks promised spacious, cheap homes. Abandoned commercial spaces seemed to cry out for the bottle coolers and clothes racks that would turn them into bars or pop-up shops. An entire airport was decommissioned, with nothing built or planted in its place, and it was initially named not Tempelhof Park, but Tempelhofer Freiheit, meaning 'freedom'. For Anna and Tom it was that space, far more than the ugly Soviet TV tower or the faux-Napoleonic Brandenburg Gate, that symbolized the true essence of Berlin: an urban void so vast that at night the rows of housing blocks on the far side looked like a shoreline viewed from the open sea – five square kilometres of pure potential. It made Anna and Tom feel almost dizzy whenever they walked across those fields. It was that potential, that abundance that had drawn them to Berlin.

Their families didn't get it. Working for themselves from home was already viewed as suspicious, a little too much like all those afternoons spent messing around on their computers after school. Their move to Berlin was frankly incomprehensible. It would have been understandable if Anna and Tom had been offered jobs there, which was why previous generations had put up with the cold climate and terrible food in West Germany. But this

31

seemed more like a whim, like a delayed study-abroad year. They suspected, correctly, that Anna and Tom topped up their income from the modest inheritance Anna's grandfather had left her to be used as a down-payment on an apartment. At their age they were supposed to be building towards a future, and what were they doing? Throwing their time and money away.

There was little Anna or Tom could say or do to convince them otherwise, bar showing them actual proof of their incomes. His parents were the joint owners of a large clothing store; her mother was an accountant and her father a lawyer. The figures Anna and Tom shared seemed low to their parents, and yet they all knew, from the papers and from hiring trainee employees themselves, that for that unlucky generation, Anna's and Tom's incomes were above average. But given the pair earned those sums primarily from clients at home, did it not make more sense to base themselves there? Those conversations were a source of frustration for Anna and Tom, not least because whenever the subject of money came up, they only ever revealed their income before tax, a half-truth that reassured their parents but ate away at them.

Their families didn't get it, but their old friends did, and they expressed their approval through likes of their pictures of the canal, the abandoned airport and the honey-coloured floorboards. Whenever Anna and Tom went home for the holidays, they would regale their old crew with stories of cheap rents and epic parties. They also began to detect a hint of provincial insularity – something they had never noticed before, presumably because those views used to be part of the natural order of things. The longer they lived in Germany, the more mindboggling southern European inefficiency seemed to them. It wasn't like that in Berlin, they would tell their friends, not out of snobbery, but in a genuine attempt to get them to move there too. And those friends would fantasize about going to visit them or following in their footsteps. They, too, longed for something else, a difference they couldn't find at home; they, too, felt that need for abundance.

Those same friends would do unpaid internships at big publishing houses, graphic design studios or creative agencies. Eventually they would get paid traineeships, maternity covers and then permanent contracts. Some of them got mortgages. They either remained in the neighbourhood where they had grown up or moved to a cheaper one out in the suburbs. All this seemed to prove Anna's and Tom's parents right, and brought on a nagging sense of insecurity whenever the pair found themselves back in town, sleeping in their friends' spare rooms or on sofa beds. But all that self-doubt would disperse like fog when they thought about their life back in Berlin. The kind of adulting called to mind by their families and so painstakingly staged by their friends followed another generation's script. Even with their regular salaries, their friends from home still earned less than Anna and Tom, two freelancers – at least in a good month. Plus, they were still stuck socializing with the same people from school. They still lived in the city where they were born. On the rare occasions they were required to speak English, it was broken and stilted. A company takeover would have put them out of a job, whereas Anna and Tom had an entire network of international contacts they could call on. Of course, their friends were not to blame, but over time that confined life of habit had sapped them of any initiative or curiosity.

In the end Anna and Tom would convince themselves that they were the ones really building towards something – something as yet hypothetical but that became more and more tangible as the months passed. After a few days of overeating and underworking, they would always be relieved to return to Berlin. They loved their families and were nostalgic for the streets they had grown up on, but that fondness would quickly give way to a feeling of stasis and estrangement. Entering the departures terminal, each time they would glance at themselves in the glass doors and think back to the picture they had taken when they left. The comparison never failed to move them. They were so different now.

The friends they made in Berlin were mostly French, Polish, Portuguese, sometimes Israeli or Belgian, occasionally American, but almost never German. They were all roughly their age – older than twenty-three, younger than thirty. They had come to the city for no particular reason and found each other as effortlessly as kids on the first day of school: meeting on Facebook groups where people swapped battered old sofas and tips to navigate German bureaucracy; or asking to borrow a laptop charger in a café with vintage formica tables and lush banyan trees; or in clubs as they waited for the bathroom, where people would leave the cubicles in twos or threes, their pupils enormous. They all had related professions. They were graphic designers and front-end developers and artists who eked out a living either working for other artists, dabbling in graphic design or mounting plasterboard booths at art fairs. They were video makers and head chefs, gallery assistants and freelance journalists leveraging Berlin's aura to imbue their articles back home with a touch of worldly sophistication. They were PhD candidates in molecular biology, musicians, copywriters and illustrators who huddled together against the winter and formed an unofficial network, an invented community. The form that community took was more of a lattice than a circle, with relationships based on affinity and emulation, affection, intimacy, similarity, Schadenfreude and support.

They had their rituals, their common references. Bloody Marys with potato latkes on Saturday mornings on Weinbergsweg. Burgers under the U-Bahn overpass on Skalitzer Straße and that other joint in the middle of nowhere, run by and for Americans, which served a burger so big it was free to whoever could finish it. They would sing ironic renditions of Oasis at karaoke beneath the Wall, watch the sun go down from the little fortress in Viktoriapark or from the Wasserturm. They would read culture and lifestyle articles written in that elegant, easy style of Anglophone magazines, which they identified with even as they ridiculed a particularly American obsession with money. In the evenings they would gravitate towards the same cluster of streets – the pedestrian bridges over the Landwehrkanal around Maybachufer, the leafy avenues in Schillerkiez, the first few blocks of Weserstraße. They would crack the same jokes about Winterdepression and the fact that they had never been to West Berlin, even though they all lived between Rixdorf and Kreuzkölln. To newcomers, almost like an initiation rite, they would pass down the rumour that the swans under Admiralbrücke were the souls of some Spanish Erasmus students who drowned in the canal during their first winter, fooled by the ice on its surface.

They would spend long weekends together that would start on Saturday mornings and run into the following afternoon. Their group would expand and contract like a living, breathing thing. The morning crew would start small, with more and more people trickling in to play table tennis in Arkonaplatz or bocce on Paul-Lincke-Ufer. They would play absent-mindedly – sometimes competing in teams, but usually all together, loosely orbiting the table and taking turns to have a go. The losers would wander off among the market stalls to browse acetate tracksuit bottoms, jars of home-made granola and funny-shaped cacti. Once the group had reconvened, they would go and get eggs and salmon (or asparagus, when it was in season) in some café, where they might stay for thirty minutes or several hours, leafing through magazines they had already read online and commenting – with barely disguised sarcasm, with suppressed rage, with nostalgia or disappointment – on the latest news from France or Portugal. The late afternoon would be spent going from gallery to gallery. They were all signed up to the same newsletter listing the latest art events, which included icons to denote whether there would be free drinks or if the crowd would be mostly German- or English-speaking. Having exhausted the openings on offer that day, some of their friends would slope off home, but they knew they would pick up others along the way – people who had spent the morning at the Turkish market, maybe, or gone for food at one of the Thai street-food stands in Preußenpark.

You could tell a gallery from all the way up the street by the little huddles of people under a neon glow, by the empties piled up around plastic beer crates on the pavement. They would spend a few minutes wandering through the gallery space and commenting on the works in whispered Greek or English – which were interesting, which derivative. Then they would plan their next stop: an independent art space above a car wash in Friedrichshain; a former furniture shop on Torstraße; the basement gallery on Graefestraße whose parties were so notoriously packed with new arrivals that it was nicknamed 'the Italian Embassy'. They would plan their route and set off, leaving any stragglers behind, confident they would catch up again somewhere along the way.

Some of their friends were artists or curators, meaning for them such occasions were professional opportunities. They would pop up among random groups like mayoral candidates on the campaign trail, dishing out compliments and handshakes. But for the rest of them, contemporary art was not, strictly speaking, a passion. Over time they might have learned how to talk the talk, but Anna and Tom were aware they didn't actually 'get it'. They couldn't even say how it had come to be such a big presence in their lives. Before moving to Berlin, they had never had any interest in art, or not beyond going to see the odd big retrospective – of Hundertwasser, say, or Man Ray. And even in Berlin, if it were down to them, they wouldn't go to all those shows, just enough to keep abreast of the visual styles their clients back home would start requesting in a few years' time, when vaporwave would trickle down from the Berlin galleries to southern Europe. But that wasn't to say they were playing the game, like the people who went along to galleries with the sole purpose of networking: Anna and Tom went because art was the pulse of their life in Berlin. It kept the oxygen flowing, kept them in the loop about parties and the latest upcoming neighbourhoods, as well as giving them a sneak preview of the new arrivals from Lisbon or Palermo or Malmö. The galleries were a stage and a social hub. The more refined among their friends referred to them as '*salons*', pronounced the French way.

Those pilgrimages could last until well into the evening, and included refreshment breaks to refuel with takeaway sushi or falafel. But at each new stop, the sizeable group amassed over the afternoon would grow slimmer and more streamlined for the night ahead. By now there would rarely be anyone from the morning left, but like the Argonauts' ship, something of the original group would remain, a particular style of dress or an in-joke repeated so often it would become a sort of secret handshake. Those still standing would assess their finances and energy levels, try to convince their friends to join over text, and make a final decision over whether to hole themselves up at one of their houses for a game of Carcassonne or venture on to Renate, to Homopatik, to Sisyphos. When they got there, the group would disband in order to get past the bouncers and then reconvene under the loudspeakers or in the bathroom queue. They would move in and out of each other's radar through the early hours, somehow always finding each other in the morning, with the exception of those who had called it a night or hooked up.

Emerging into the light, which hit them like needles in their eyes, they would look for a peaceful place to let the energy wash away, cracking more jokes with hoarse voices on the U-Bahn. Sometimes they would make it all the way to Mauerpark to recover with a greasy breakfast from one of the fast-food stands. Other times, weather permitting, they would lie down to doze and drink cold-brewed yerba mate on Tempelhof's grassy expanse. They would still be drunk and high, vibratile, the bass booming on in their ears. They would imagine how they must look to the outside world with their aching cheekbones drawn into fixed grins, their clothes smeared with cigarette ash and sweat, and still carrying the odd trace of dimly remembered adventures: a marker pen scribble on their face; a garland of fake frangipani in their pocket; a bunch of helium balloons tied to their jacket buttons and now trailing, half-deflated, like comet tails. They would feel decadent and enviable, alive.

By early afternoon the first stirrings of anxiety would make themselves felt, then slowly build like a gathering storm. They would remember the supermarkets, closed on Sundays, their client calls scheduled for Monday, the work due by Friday. They would part ways without making plans and get on the U-Bahn to their one- or two-bed apartments with their plants and wooden floors, to the impending serotonin crash and the warm bath to soften the fall. They would send a few sheepish messages to assuage their guilt at some half-remembered thing they had said or done. Most of the time no one answered. They would take two aspirins before climbing into bed and by Monday morning everything would be fine, or almost everything, or almost fine.

Their friendships were surprisingly easy, but there was also something precarious and brittle about them. Anna and Tom had been welcomed with an almost suspicious level of interest and openness, proof of a loneliness everyone was trying to exorcise. It would not have occurred to them to call on those friends in times of need. There were certain topics they never talked about, like money. There was the odd sudden, unprovoked defection, but never any fully-fledged rifts – they weren't close enough to warrant actually hurting each other. Instead, the group would undergo internal realignments, opportunistic shifts in allyship. They would still bump into each other outside gallery openings, but only ever exchanged quick hellos, and it was taken as read that they wouldn't be sharing a taxi to Bar Drei.

Periodically someone would disappear. It was more common in winter. Sometimes their landlord would break the lease agreement. Sometimes they would get a job back home. And sometimes there would be no apparent reason at all. At first the friend would stop showing up at openings or replying to messages. Their German number would go straight to voicemail. Soon enough Anna and Tom would hear – either via Facebook or word of mouth – that their friend was back in Marseille, or Athens, or Copenhagen. Sometimes there would be a proper leaving party with a rented sound system and a plant auction. But more often, what was supposed to be a quick trip home would drag on for months, until the friends who had agreed to keep their bicycle for them would receive an email putting them in touch with some guy driving a van from Berlin to wherever the bicycle owner had returned. We'll definitely be back, these emails would say, as soon as we find an apartment or a job, once the PhD or the winter is over, once the baby is weaned. And the ones who had stayed would reply, See you soon, can't wait, so jealous of the warm weather down there, when really they knew their friends weren't coming back.

That sense of instability manifested as a constant nervous energy. Every winter, every weekend could be one person's last and another's first. It made Anna and Tom feel alive, fuelled their curiosity and sense of adventure, and reinforced the impression that the city was inexhaustible. And yet their world was smaller now than it had been when they were students. At any given time there were, at most, a dozen or so people they saw on a regular basis, and the liminal circle of vaguely familiar faces and half-acquaintances was looser and more ill-defined than it had been at university. Not that they ever noticed, because that limited world regenerated fast enough to give the illusion of infinity.

Every so often Anna and Tom would choose to spend the weekend by themselves, to recover from a run of late nights or simply to enjoy each other's company alone. They would spend the morning in bed leafing through magazines and scrolling social media, then pop out for bagels still wearing their pyjamas. In the afternoon they might go for a walk, but usually they would stay at home to nap, listen to music, fuck. As evening fell they would realize they had been on their own, just the two of them, for more than twenty-four hours. It would feel good.

The house would be clean and tidy. Their deadlines would be under control. The fridge would be full but they would order in Vietnamese anyway. They would light candles and pour rice noodles from their foil containers into enamel bowls. Every now and then their phones would light up with an invitation or plan, to which they would respond that they felt like being alone, or else gave no response at all. From down on the street the muffled sound of people joking in Turkish or German would meld with the instrumental post-rock on their record player. Tourists would pause briefly under the warm tungsten glow of the streetlamps to look for something in their pockets.

In moments like these, everything seemed possible. They could look back and see they had pretty much everything they had ever wished for. It had been easy, but also difficult. They knew they had been lucky to find each other so young, but it had also taken determination and perseverance. They didn't feel they had missed out on much. They were in love.

The results of that love were all around them. Delicious hot meals, their bills paid, a job and home they liked – the details that comprised their life. It was a life they had created for themselves, building difference upon difference until it encapsulated the real them, with a freedom they would never have had back at home. They were proud of it. On the other side of the window the city pulsed on, calling them with promises they were in no rush to put to the test.

Later on they would fall asleep breathing in each other's smell, whispering little jokes, sweet nothings, plans for the next day. But really what they were saying was a prayer, a silent and strangely solemn prayer for things to remain exactly as they were. It was always answered.

Their love grew deeper every day. They were lovers, partners, best friends. The connection they first felt at university had only strengthened over the course of their foreign adventure. Minor betrayals had been forgiven or left unsaid. Through the strains of everyday life, they had learned to rely on each other. Tom called Anna's parents without fail once a week; Anna wrote his emails in German for him. They had a joint Volksbank account but separate Netflix profiles, although the algorithm suggested the same shows for both of them. Either of them could choose anything on their joint behalf – be it a dish from a menu or an apartment – without a second thought, confident that the other would like it. They would fight over silly things: random social media storms, a form they were supposed to fill in. Every other Sunday they would clean the apartment while listening to old Eurovision songs. They never doubted they would grow old together. The sex was infrequent and bad.

Or at least that's what they feared. It might be a Friday night and they would have arrived home freezing cold and high from a housewarming in Charlottenburg or Wedding. It might be a Sunday morning, too early to get out of bed, but with the summer sun already up and warming the room through the blackout curtain. The possibility would hang in the air – perhaps it had been a week since the last time, or they both glimpsed an opportunity – and a gesture by one of them would awaken that possibility in the other. Without undressing, Anna would press her crotch against Tom's hip, pinning his wrists down onto the mattress so that he couldn't touch her with his cold hands. Or Tom would test to see if she was awake by running a hand softly, almost imperceptibly, down her back, and then slipping it under the elastic of her knickers. A back would arch, a neck would roll to one side.

Tom would first use his fingers, then go down on her until she came, which happened just often enough to constitute being often enough. Sometimes he would use the lightest possible touch, deliberately slowing down when he could see her cheeks start to flush. Sometimes he would run the tip of his tongue over and around her clitoris before sliding one finger inside her, then another. Sometimes she would ask him to take her from behind but to stay absolutely still, just kissing her neck while she slowly gyrated her hips and touched herself from the front with her eyes closed. They might be on the yoga mat. They might be in the shower. Anna would come first, or, less commonly, give up trying, which he would take as permission to let go and come within seconds, in a condom, on the bedsheets or in the pool of water that collected around the drain.

That routine was perfected fairly early on in their relationship, and had always satisfied them. If ever one of them wasn't in the mood, the other would understand without getting offended or feeling rejected. On the other hand, if one of them got horny during the working day, the other would play along and let themselves be dragged onto the sofa, or tease them for a while, pretending to be very absorbed in their work. The whole thing could take five minutes or half an hour. Afterwards, one of them would sit on the other's lap, their skin covered in goosebumps. Or they would both get straight out of bed to make breakfast in the nude, the smell of sex still clinging to their bodies. Or they would cuddle in the dark feeling sleep approach and listening in silence to the other's breathing. And for a moment they would feel happy, close.

The moment would pass. A thought would worm its way into that bliss: that was the same sex they'd had last week, two months ago, three years ago. Looking at it objectively, it probably was on the short side. And unimaginative, perhaps? Anal sex didn't do it for either of them. Anna had been curious about rimming but Tom was too self-conscious. He wasn't crazy about blowjobs, but he did like to be choked just before coming, which Anna found a bit scary. They would climax once and then call it a day, lie in each other's arms and silently wonder: Shouldn't they fuck more often, come harder? What were they missing out on by dismissing toys and sex clubs and BDSM? Had they ruled out polyamory because it wasn't for them, or because they were priggish and scared?

The world around them offered such an exciting image of how their sex life could be. Social media accounts dedicated to sex positivity endorsed rings and plugs, bullets and vibrators, and silicone strap-ons of all shapes and sizes in shiny chrome or pastel colours. Their friends would talk about the emotional arbitration involved in poly relationships or scroll through their joint Tinder, checking out potential candidates for a threesome that weekend. The ads that would appear between the paragraphs of the online lifestyle articles they read would be for colourful marble-effect dildos shaped like tigers and dragons. At the clubs they went to, women with shocking pink or bright green hair and dressed in skimpy strips of nylon fishnet would proffer their boots for worship to strangers wrapped in latex and patent leather; there would be couples and threesomes cosied up on sofas, exchanging propositions and clear plastic baggies before disappearing off towards the darkrooms or VIP booths. The mood would be playful, euphoric, full of intrigue; they were all so uninhibited and gorgeous, or that was what it looked like. They also seemed to be having a lot more fun than Anna and Tom.

And when the moment passed they would still be thinking about that fun, as they lay wrapped up in their cosy bathrobes or nestled under the herringbone blanket, listening to each other's breathing. They couldn't put their finger on exactly what it was they craved, but they knew it was very different to what they had. An entire erotic world lay just out of reach, closed off to them – so closed off that they couldn't even say what it was that they were missing. They were happy with their sex life, and when they talked about it they said as much, and believed it. In a way, this was what was so suspicious. They worried they were content merely being contented.

They knew any dissatisfaction they felt wasn't owing to how long they'd been together, or to their relative lack of sexual experience when they met. Polyamory wasn't for them – and not only because their friends' exploits made it seem like a bureaucratic and ultimately humiliating arrangement, but because they were good together. They understood each other, liked each other, and if ever they did let each other down, it was usually over something minor and foreseeable. They felt rather pathetic being so comfortable with long-term monogamy, but the truth was they were rarely attracted to other people, and even then it was always fleeting. They would point those people out to each other in bars or at parties, but it never went further than spinning fantasies they'd later act out in bed. They wouldn't have wanted to experiment with anyone else; they could never have felt the same level of trust, the same openness to play. And they were reassured by this fact, but at the same time disheartened by it.

Every once in a while, they would buy a toy. One of them would read a piece by a New York journalist about how she'd taught her boyfriend to use a double strap-on, and then send the affiliate link to the other over Slack. Or they would be seduced by a professional-quality video made by some influencer demonstrating a clitoral stimulator on a citrus fruit. On their walks they would find themselves drawn to the refined minimalism of new sex shops, such a far cry from the flashy, lurid feel to the ones back home. Of course they would go in, attracted like moths to the neon lights glowing between those white plasterboard walls. They would wander around the displays, hyperaware of the sales assistant's presence, playing at being the kind of couple who knew enough about vibrators to compare them. They would loiter for a few minutes, relishing that image of themselves even if it didn't really suit them. Then, more than anything to curb the feeling that they were imposters, they would buy something: a travel rabbit or a cock ring or some sustainably produced lube made with CBD oil.

They used those purchases rarely, and never for long enough for their awkwardness to relax into spontaneity. Once they had removed it from its packaging, charged and washed it, they would leave their new toy in plain sight on the bedside table, where they would eye it uneasily for a couple of days until the next time one of them reached over for a condom and thought: why not? They weren't embarrassed – together they laughed at their inexperience, guided each other – but their awkwardness prevented them from really enjoying those toys: the harness would be either too loose or so tight their leg went dead; the bullet would get stuck in the silicone and they would have to squeeze it out to reach the button. The buzzing would put them off their stride. And the constant questioning – were they using it correctly, was it all going as it was supposed to – far from opening up new possibilities, dampened their pleasure. The stimulation made Anna come quickly, but in truth she preferred

Tom going down on her, because she thought that was what Tom preferred. Tom was into the idea of a plug, but whenever they tried it, it hurt too much. After showering, they would clean their new purchase with a special disinfectant to be used a few more times, at ever longer intervals, until finally they would put it away in the tin beside Anna's pillow with all the other toys that radiated waves of dissatisfaction over their bed.

Every so often those waves would propel them towards a sex club. It was never planned. They might be in a taxi heading home from a party that had ended too early, and as they waited at the lights on Heinrich-Heine-Straße, their eyes would be caught by a gate with a queue stretching all the way around the block. Or they might have a few drinks over dinner and get turned on by a scene in a film, or by the conversation, or just because, and it would be a Friday or Saturday and they'd say to themselves: Why not? It didn't happen often.

And so they would find themselves in line, surrounded by tattooed and half-naked bodies in the freezing cold: people in skin-tight latex tube dresses, fishnet tops, plugs, studs, leather chokers, fluorescent wigs, leotards, high heels, garters. Next to them, Anna and Tom would feel very plain, but also turned on. Once again, they would promise themselves they would go out and buy something suitable for the dress code. But they never had any trouble getting past the door, because they were a couple and looked sufficiently cool and weren't too high and could mutter something in passable German. Once inside that throbbing semi-darkness, they would immediately head for the bar, then dance together in stilted, jerking moves until they felt drunk and brave enough to move over to the poolside sofas or the mezzanine floor where people would lounge around smoking. From there they would look around.

Eventually a single guy or couple would approach the pair of them, or a woman might give Anna the eye. All the women had dilated pupils and all the men had hair matted with wax and sweat. They would chat in English, say a little about themselves, how long they'd been in Berlin, whether they were a couple, open or closed, straight or bi. Anna and Tom always said bi, even though he had never been with a man and she only once with a woman, with Tom also there: they'd sent her home, apologizing, straight after, and Anna never called the number she found in her pocket the next morning.

The propositions would inevitably come: a word whispered in an ear would become a little suck on an earlobe, or a friendly hand on a shoulder would slide down into a caress. Shins rubbed against shins, fingers interlaced, a pair of knees would part almost imperceptibly. The music would drum in their heads, and through the smoke and strobe lights everyone seemed interesting and mysterious. Anna and Tom would exchange a look. The air would smell of sweat and tobacco, of sugar and disinfectant. Their hearts would be beating both faster and slower.

It was hard to say why they didn't ever end up doing anything. The urge they felt in those moments was very strong, blinding – whether it was desire or more a desire to desire – but every time, without fail, something stopped them. It could be the middle-aged man who followed them to watch, or the sobbing and moaning of the woman teetering on the edge of a k-hole. Tom could be put off by the sight of a half-limp dick blossoming from a cock ring. For Anna it could be someone going in to kiss her collarbone too roughly; she would recoil from the smell of musk and secretions and a scratchy beard, and feel very far away. Seen in isolation, those moments of hesitation in the chill-out area or darkroom were perfectly legitimate, but together they represented something more: a vague sense of shame that they couldn't put a name to but that was always lurking, ready to make itself felt. They would return to the dancefloor with the excuse of needing a drink, or sometimes without any excuse at all.

Despite almost crossing the threshold several times, in the end they always found themselves back in line for the coat room. They would be tired and smelly, but their unease would fade the second they stepped out into the cool night air. If a taxi passed they might hail it. Otherwise they would walk home in the grey light of dawn, hands clasped, exhilarated, unified. And also, in truth, relieved to have spared themselves the STD tests, glad they hadn't accepted those water bottles, baggies and vials. Once in bed, their excitement would soften into tenderness. They would spoon under the covers, let their breathing fall in sync and tell themselves that no sex party could ever be a match for the intimacy and gratification of that closeness.

In the morning that thought would seem pathetic.

They lived a double life. There was the tangible reality around them, and there were the images, also all around them.

Those images would be on the phone that woke them up. An astronaut singing in outer space. A girl riding a wrecking ball. They would light up their pillows as they roused from sleep, and parade, one after the other, beneath their fingertips while they used the bathroom. They would be there in the kitchen on the tablet as Anna and Tom waited for their coffee to brew, then reappear seamlessly on their monitors in the home office. A jealous husband's threats graffitied across the front of a house. Goats teetering on a cliffside or at the edge of a motorway flyover. Whenever they went out for lunch, the images would shrink to the size of the rectangular screen and hover, mid-air, a foot above their plates. A tornado of sharks in the sky. While they waited for the U8 or the M29. While they took a piss. A famous woman spraying an arc of champagne backwards over her head into a wine glass balanced on her tailbone. Those images lit up their faces in the dark bedroom when they went to set the alarm. The faces of strangers. The faces of handsome criminals. Avocado slices.

Working at their computers, the images would blow in like a storm through the windows left open in the background. They would send an invoice and check their Instagram. The latest polls in the upcoming elections back home would vie for their attention with a flashing notification in the browser tab. The keyboard shortcut to jump from one tab to the next was etched onto their muscle memory, like Command-C, Command-V. They would scour Stack Exchange for the parameters of a particularly clunky CSS class and steal a look at a discussion begun earlier on Facebook. Just below that, their attention would shift to an ad for a Spanish- and English-speaking tax consultant in Berlin. In the comments, a loose acquaintance would be claiming it was a scam. Her profile would catch their eye. They would send a friendship request and discover she was planning to go to a night at KitKat the following week. Scrolling down the list of attendees, they would spot an old friend who used to live in Neukölln. But wasn't she back in Madrid? It certainly seemed so from her LinkedIn page. A drenched kitten. A photo essay on the US President's laid-back elegance. A selfie.

These interruptions could last two seconds or several minutes. Sometimes, when work felt particularly repetitive or a discussion concerned them personally, they could eat up whole half-hours. They couldn't have said how much time they spent like that each day. They suspected it was a lot.

It hadn't always been this way. Something must have changed for them somewhere. They just couldn't work out what.

They could still remember a time when they only used Facebook to find out what had happened to their school crushes, and when Instagram was little more than an archive of people's holiday snaps. Since then, they had followed the many evolutions of those websites from their dual perspective as both interface designers and users. They could name every single update – the introduction of likes and notifications, video sharing, picture posting, tagging. But any attempt to draw a connection between those minutiae and the way in which social media had spread through every aspect of their lives was so reductive as to miss the point entirely, like wondering whether it is at the first twig or the third tree that a forest can be said to be on fire.

They would have liked to do something about it, but quitting social media, even one platform, didn't seem possible. Coming off Facebook would have significantly reduced their social life. It had been indispensable for finding friends and establishing networks in Berlin, and was the main source of all the practical information they could need. It was also the last remaining open channel to their old lives. They didn't often talk to people back home – perhaps the constant, spectral presence of that stream of images eliminated that need – but reading about their promotions and newborns and seeing pictures of their class reunions made Anna and Tom feel that they were still somehow a part of their lives.

They weren't so into Twitter, even if it did sometimes make them laugh, but it was their main source of news from their country. An interest in home affairs had survived their move abroad, while they'd never taken any notice of German news, which was all in German. If they quit Twitter, they would only go back to refreshing newspaper and magazine homepages every hour, getting less personalized information and wasting even more time. Instagram was a showcase for their work as well as being a constant source of new ideas and inspiration. Quitting Instagram was out of the question.

Even their attempts to restrict their use to specific times of the day or to impose a daily limit proved futile. It wasn't down to boredom or an inability to concentrate. In fact, it was often while getting on with the most creative parts of their job – brainstorming a pitch or coming up with a new grid – that they would plunge headfirst into the flow of images for a few minutes, emerging recharged, focused.

And yet they were embarrassed about how much time they spent on there. Tom had positioned his monitor at an angle to avoid it being reflected in the windows of the office they shared. Whenever he got up to go to the loo or the kitchen, Anna would quickly switch desktop before he walked past. They would find themselves utterly mesmerized by the apartment, kale salad or kitten of someone living two blocks or two continents away. They would get worked up about silly fights between strangers. They would show a fervent interest in the affairs of people they would never meet.

It was like walking through the world's most hectic street market on cocaine. It was like channel hopping an entire wall of TV sets. It was like telepathically tuning into the thoughts of a stadium packed with people. But really it wasn't like anything else, because it was new.

Even their moods were new, which is why they had no commonly recognized name. Instead, they would be described in terms borrowed from other, vaguely related types of experiences, all of which fell short of expressing an inner landscape reconfigured by twenty years of the internet.

The shame they felt at their lack of self-control was really a failure on their part to adapt their thinking to the changing environment. They still thought of their days in terms of a central activity – work – and a constellation of distractions. But on closer inspection, this jumping from screen to screen and from window to window was actually more of a flow state. The very idea of a 'distraction' assumed a separation between the personal and the professional – between news stories and banter, project pitches and catchy pop hooks. If ever there had been such a distinction, it had long since evaporated. They would drift from one thing to the other because one thing *was* the other. On social media, just as on InDesign, time disappeared.

These new emotions weren't all negative. What was

that rush they would get after a particularly popular post? And the itch that made them look up from their work every twenty seconds, every minute, to refresh the page and watch the number of likes clock up, as if it were a stock ticker or a scoreboard? They felt it every day, and yet that feeling had no name. It wasn't a scoreboard – there was no prize at the end. Financially speaking, it had very little impact, if any. Fifty-year-old sociologists would talk about narcissism, but they were only talking about themselves. Pop-neuroscience journalists would write about it in terms of drug and sugar addiction and depression. Anna and Tom knew these were the oversimplified conclusions of technophobes. They didn't see it like that. But they would have conceded that it wasn't *not* like that.

When that woman posted a racist comment about AIDS, Anna and Tom spent the entire day obsessively following the fallout, forgetting about their work, just as the driver who slows down to gawp at a road accident forgets where he's driving to. The pictures. The comment pieces. The comments beneath the comment pieces. The screenshots of comments now deleted, whether out of fear they might look bad or a genuine sense of shame. The screenshots of headlines so disgraceful they didn't merit a link to the article. Everyone would google them anyway. But why?

Finding their way out of the ethical jungle was compelling, like trying to solve an impossible riddle. The racist joke was, indeed, appalling. Losing face, not to mention one's livelihood, in front of millions of strangers was unfair. There was a price to be paid for bigotry. Mob mentality was to be avoided. In the future, people would be publicly shamed for any minor slip-up. In the future, being publicly shamed would be so common it would stop being an effective deterrent. All the different perspectives seemed valid, and there was always someone to back them up. Why were they so interested in that woman's story? Did it interest them as news or as a novel? Did it interest them because they saw themselves in her? Did it interest them because they saw themselves in her accusers?

Anna and Tom's conversations flowed seamlessly between the digital and the physical domains. They would post on each other's timelines and discuss the stories over their monitors while they worked. Sometimes they would burst out laughing at exactly the same time, having been fed the same meme on their feeds. Their comments on the issues of the day would be commented on by their friends, to whom Anna and Tom would then email links to thinkpieces arguing the opposite. Five minutes later, those friends would come back with a new thread. They also worked with the windows open. The storms also blew into their apartments.

In the evenings, at the Biergarten on Paul-Lincke-Ufer or in the Russian bistro under the Wasserturm, they would often end up discussing things they had seen online, which was to say somewhere in the world, which usually meant in California or New York. Their fundamental positions wouldn't have changed, but something in the tone of the discussion would have. Differences of opinion that, online, were expressed in sarcastic retorts and subtweets would feel far less extreme in person. Somehow, value systems that seemed completely incompatible on social feeds could find a middle ground around a table at a café. They would no longer smack so hard of toxic masculinity, or Eurocentrism, or privilege. The discussion would peter out into a joke, into an order for another round of drinks. Within a day or two, they would forget all about it.

But polemics and current affairs were mere thunder and lightning in what was otherwise a deluge of beauty. On their screens – everywhere, all the time – acquaintances and old schoolmates and strangers from around the world would share all that was beautiful in their lives. The images followed no logical thread beyond their own splendour: vintage clothes and filtered selfies, snow-covered forests, crystalline coastlines, bright, airy apartments, book covers, cupcakes, flowers, wild animals, galaxies, contemporary art shows, feet. Anna and Tom would be captivated. Their interest in plants – a hobby that had never occurred to them when they were students – was likely a result of the never-ending stream of pictures they were fed of stunning plants in bay windows, on plywood shelves, against herringbone parquet. The bright green tropical leaves and the purplish-white dots on the begonias would parade across photo grids as evidence of a rarefied, curated life. Anna and Tom didn't notice the change until after it had happened. Plants appeared out of nowhere, a fully developed skill.

Something similar had happened with cooking. When had it started? At university they hadn't given much thought to food. They could whip up a few family favourites, but mostly ate fast food or sandwiches. The pinnacle of culinary talent was knowing how to feed the eight or so course mates who would meet up on Sunday for study sessions – a big pot of soup, a curry, spaghetti Bolognese. Salty, stodgy meals, high in calories and all the same reddish-brown colour. They would serve them on mismatched blue and pistachio IKEA plates. The portions were always very generous.

They cringed to think of it now. Their screens had unlocked a whole world of differences they hadn't even known existed. Dark bluish-green kale and shiny emerald avocados would leap out against white enamel plates with a blue trim or light grey handmade ceramic bowls garnished with pomegranate seeds and flecks of balsamic glaze. The matte finish of a slate slab would beautifully set off bright curls of fresh cheese sprinkled with herbs and halved grapes. The dishes would include a scattering of seeds, studied swirls of sauce and little pearls of reduction. Vegetables would be stir-fried in a carbon steel pan that was later wiped with grapeseed oil, never washed; risottos simmered not in an ancient pressure cooker but in a heavy-bottomed sauteuse; soups and stews demanded the very particular thermal qualities and materiality of clay terrines and cast-iron casseroles. Sous-vide cookers would bring out the texture and tenderness of rare cuts of meat – hanger steak, tongue. Seeds would be toasted, sauces blended, at least partly, for creaminess. Kohlrabi and trombetta zucchini and greenish-yellow heirloom tomatoes would be sliced into impossibly thin slivers or rustic chunks on thick butcher's blocks. Their preferred knives were first ceramic, then rusty Vietnamese steel, then forged stainless steel.

Anna and Tom devoted a lot of mental energy to this passion, which seemed to have developed out of nowhere, but fully formed. They also devoted considerable expense to it. It wasn't consumerism that drove them, however; they had no desire to show off any particular brand of tableware or luxury foodstuff. They favoured simple ingredients whose flavours they could elevate with the right preparation, just as the white enamel plates could bring out the gold-studded purple of a caramelized beetroot. Their interest hadn't been planted by sly marketers, but appeared as if by osmosis, as they observed the little differences all around them. It was part of their quest for freedom and pleasure – the pleasure of eating, chiefly, but also the tactile pleasure of cooking slowly, and the visual pleasure afforded by the perfect plating.

All their friends shared this interest. Mysteriously enough, they had discovered home-made fermentation kits, fire-roasted cauliflower and umami at exactly the same time as Anna and Tom. As they had grown older, the nights out – drug-hazed nights spent sandwiched between tourists – had been gradually replaced by lazy lunches on summer afternoons or candlelit dinners behind frost-covered windowpanes.

On those occasions, reclaimed wooden tables would be laid with raw cotton tablecloths and tin or amber glass plates, themselves filled with elaborate salads sprinkled with seeds and fruit, quinoa and fava beans, or seasonal roasted root vegetables seasoned with ginger and sumac. Wedges of chèvre or fossa would gleam beneath a glass cheese dome. IPAs from local microbreweries would slosh in earthenware steins, while the spent yeast sediment from the natural wine would sit at the bottom of thin-stemmed glasses. The smell of freshly ground, single-origin, lightly roasted coffee would waft from chunky brown and white porcelain cups.

Each course would be accompanied by a chorus of compliments and technical remarks, or else by an embarrassed explanation of what had gone wrong. The conversation would revolve around food markets, bakeries and cooking times in electric versus gas ovens. On their way home from these dinner parties, Anna and Tom would review every detail of the dishes they had been served, though not in a spirit of competition. They were all learning together. Food was part of their culture, and they would discuss it among themselves in the same way previous generations had discussed films, books and politics. It helped define who they were.

The most striking dishes would be photographed, tagged and shared. Those images would then travel to the other end of the planet, bouncing along in low Earth orbit or speeding across ocean ridges, reaching the screens of their peers in Lyon, Helsinki and Valencia, who would look at them for a moment, entranced by the differences, before pressing a keyboard shortcut etched into their muscle memory, and getting back to work at a café with decent wifi, daily specials on a blackboard and sprawling aloe plants. An egg became more famous than the Pope. A highly contagious virus raged through West Africa. A billionaire poured a bucket of ice on his head. A fashion brand exploited East Asian sweatshop workers. A young woman recorded all the times she was catcalled. Two African Americans were killed by the police. A man went around filming first kisses. A plane vanished en route to Beijing. A woman was beautiful. An apartment full of plants was beautiful. A vegan quiche was beautiful. A child needed money for chemo. Time disappeared.

The city ebbed and flowed like a tide. Winter would bring the usual flurry of defections, and spring a fresh wave of expats. New venues and galleries would open and become increasingly crowded until even newer ones replaced them. Anna and Tom slowly climbed the ranks of legitimacy. They spoke better German than most. They were the ones offering up their address to newcomers needing to register an Anmeldung and handing out tips on how to join the Künstlersozialkasse. They passed on the felt insoles that had stopped them getting frostbite the first winter. They looked forward to Brandenburg Airport opening so they could reminisce about Tegel with the same cool superiority as the veteran expats who reminisced about their first flights into Tempelhof.

Fewer and fewer of the new arrivals would be from Spain, France and Italy, and more and more from Bavaria and the US. In addition to the usual musicians and graduate students, lots of these people worked in finance or tech. They either had permanent jobs or regular freelance contracts with start-ups based in the Pacific Time Zone. They still worked from cafés like everyone else, but that new row of luminescent apples emanated an intense concentration altogether distinct from the dreamy, distracted atmosphere of before. Those newcomers didn't wear garish headphones throbbing with electropop, but sleek, noise-cancelling earbuds. They got annoyed at people smoking at the next table. They posted reviews of bars criticizing the roast level on the coffee blend or the internet upload speed.

A new spirit seemed to manifest itself in a thousand tiny details. Gourmet hamburger joints were popping up everywhere. Bedbugs, previously only a problem in the US, were on the rise in neighbourhoods all over the city, with dermatologists mapping spikes in cases on streets with a higher concentration of short-term lettings. New restaurants were staffed by Scottish or Australian bartenders and only had menus in English. The old regulars would remark bitterly that no one even attempted to learn German anymore. Anna and Tom, on the other hand, loved that vague Anglophone displacement. It was precisely what made them feel at home.

Their English wasn't perfect, but they could more than get by. English was the glue that held their community together, with variants and mistakes tolerated so that everyone felt free to speak. Until such time as someone claimed English as theirs – and there were still too few Londoners and New Yorkers for that – it belonged to everyone. So accustomed were they to the mishmash of French, Italian and Polish accents, they found it harder to understand Irish English than the drunk Spaniards' lispy Spanglish. When they hung out in groups they would switch seamlessly between their own language and a heavily accented English punctuated with German terms pronounced in a faintly Californian drawl.

Language wasn't the only national trait to dissolve. They had stopped reading newspapers from home soon after moving, the moment they realized how sloppy the journalism was compared to the writing in their English-language equivalents. Their intellectual horizon was therefore largely formed from headlines in the *Guardian* or the *New York Times*, which happened to be the same newspapers their Greek, Dutch and Belgian friends read. In their world, Barack Obama's speeches and high school shootings existed far more vividly than the laws passed just a few U-Bahn stations away, or the refugees drowning two hours' flight south.

News and language created a sort of shared ideological koine. They and all their friends belonged to an imprecise political left. They identified as feminists and spoke out against social injustices, which in practice meant they were willing to express outrage at instances of racism or sexism that took place in New York. Anna and Tom had publicly distanced themselves from a client which refused to publicly distance itself from a sexist ad. They donated ten dollars a month to a foundation supporting LGBTQ rights, which came to just under nine dollars after the Californian payment platform took its commission. Like their friends, they were unsure whether to admire Hillary Clinton as a woman or despise her for her ties to the pharmaceutical industry. Of course, all that was theoretical; in practice, their social commitment amounted to using Uber only if it was snowing and always leaving tips in cash. They didn't eat tuna.

The influx of native English speakers was increasing, but it went largely unnoticed. They seemed to dilute in the general Anglophony, just another accent among many. Little weight was given to the fact that the lingua franca was starting to belong to some more than others. The Americans were not the least surprised to turn up in a foreign capital and find a readymade community of people there to welcome them and discuss their country's politics in their language. Why would they be? They felt at home in Berlin. They, too, did their best to avoid using Uber. They, too, were conflicted about Hillary Clinton.

An obsession with real estate – imported by the New Yorkers, together with the bedbugs – dominated conversation. Everyone was looking for a better apartment and a fairer deal, or they wanted to know how much others were paying and the terms of their contract. All this would have seemed utterly irrelevant just a few years earlier, when the choice for renters was between vast apartments for six hundred euros a month and tiny ones for two-twenty. The injection of dollars, which could buy more metres in Berlin than feet in San Francisco, only fuelled the chaos in the city's housing market. Every week, Anna and Tom would receive at least two emails asking if they knew of anyone leaving an apartment, or if they had any leads. The senders were almost always strangers, and from the email subject lines it was clear the request had been forwarded in a chain going back weeks. Over brunches at home or at gallery openings they would trade information on the documents required to qualify for rent control – WBS, Sonderbedarf – and discuss whether it was worth paying for membership to the tenants' union. They would enter the technical terms from their rental contracts into Google Translate. They would think back to when units in new builds went on sale for three thousand euros a square metre and everyone laughed at the accountants from Stuttgart and the dentists from Milan for paying so much for their tiny slice of an infinite city. They weren't laughing now.

Evictions were also becoming more common. At first, Anna and Tom weren't especially concerned. To them, squats and other occupied spaces had a quaint but ultimately outdated appeal, part of a vision – belonging to the eighties – of the city as a gritty, conflict-torn place. And in any case, Berlin was so full of those spaces that a degree of friction seemed inevitable. They were, though, shaken by the demolition of Tacheles, the turn-of-the-century department store that had been an art squat and cultural venue for two decades. In truth, they had only been a few times – that graffiti aesthetic seemed painfully naive compared to the Berlin Bienniale just a few streets away. During their first months, though, making their way to the Boros art bunker or that pizza restaurant set in an old ballroom, they would be struck by the beauty of the place. The stucco cornices bearing layer upon layer of posters and DJ booths set up behind lavish glazed arches perfectly embodied the abundance and freedom that made Berlin unique. They had fully intended to be at the protest, but at the last minute they'd had to jump on a client call, and that neighbourhood was quite a long way away. It was only months later, when they happened to be on Oranienburger Straße, that they saw, to their astonishment, how quickly Tacheles had been destroyed.

Not even the old airport was safe. The survival of a vast, essentially vacant plot right in the heart of the city had for a long time been taken as a sign of Berlin's resistance to speculation. But the announcement of a new building project – earmarking the space partly for subsidized housing and partly for luxury apartments – sounded a warning impossible to ignore. The response was immediate and widespread, with both long-time residents of the area and the French, Spanish and American newcomers all getting behind the cause, since the leaflets were in English and German. Some wanted the space to be inalienably preserved as a green space, but others (predominantly Berliners) were in favour of the development, which would increase the public housing stock. The plan to build a kilometre-high artificial mountain there for an inner-city ski resort got a lot of attention before it was exposed as a prank. The referendum had prompted an unprecedented outpouring of civic consciousness within Anna and Tom's circles, even if not all of them could vote in it, because to do so you had to be a tax resident. The results had been ambiguous – the proposed projects were all rejected but no binding future resolution was passed. For Anna and Tom, this lack of plan didn't represent defeat. It was far better for Tempelhof to remain exactly as it was: a reservoir of potential futures.

What was happening to the city – the replacement of its historical inhabitants with younger, wealthier newcomers, and the resulting price hikes and decline in diversity – was gentrification, a term used almost exclusively by the people who caused it. Anna and Tom were fully aware of this. They drank in bars where a craft beer cost three times as much as a Pils in a local Eckkneipe; they loitered outside art gallery windowfronts still bearing the original 1980s neon shop signs advertising the second-hand goods dealers and shoemakers they had pushed out; the previous tenants of their apartment had paid their rent in marks. They realized they had contributed to the problem that was starting to affect them, but they knew it in an unacknowledged, almost imperceptible way, like smokers when they think about cancer. Back when they had first arrived, things still cost very little. The shoe repairmen were in business until the Americans showed up. Gentrification, as they understood it, was something other people did.

It did occur to them that, had they arrived now, they probably wouldn't have found an apartment as good as theirs, or not one they could afford. Sometimes this realization prompted a flicker of anxiety, as if the solid life they had built was merely an accident of timing. There were moments when they felt their identity was anchored not in their thoughts or deeds, but in something fickle and brittle, a roll of the dice.

In such moments they would feel hopeless. It could be a Sunday afternoon at home, already dark at four, with an icy wind lashing sleet and hail against the windows. Their eyes would be sore from too many hours spent staring at a screen. A client from back home could have failed to pay them. The Hausverwaltung could have raised their rent without any explanation. The Finanzamt might be late in issuing that year's Ansässigkeitsbescheinigung. Spring would seem very far away, at the furthest end of an infinite repetition of days like that. They would sit down on the Scandinavian armchairs with a jasmine or fennel tea and think about how, that week, João or Émilie had also left. Deep down, they understood them.

On those days, the images of Berlin that they held so dear would blur; or rather, they would seem misleading: accurate enough within their limited scope but framed in such a way as to cut out a crucial part of the experience they were supposed to depict. In their place, in a kind of reversed perspective, memories of their university days, of the streets they knew by heart, came into their minds. If they hadn't moved abroad, that Sunday they would have gone for lunch with one of their families. They would probably still be drinking coffee around the table. It would be daylight . Though it remained unspoken, Anna and Tom would both feel the crush of nostalgia. What were they doing there? It wasn't so much their hometown that they missed, but something they had taken for granted back when they lived there. They couldn't say precisely what that something was, but its absence made daily life in Berlin feel intense, draining – more exciting, maybe, but ultimately harder.

From the outside, it was easy enough to identify the cause of their alienation, but to them, paradoxically, no explanation revealed itself. Anna and Tom lived in a bubble, one even more insular and limited than those just starting to appear on social media. In a way, they had become radicalized. They spoke stumbling English with other non-native English speakers. They inhabited a world where everyone accepted a line of coke, where no one was a doctor or a baker or a taxi driver or a middle school teacher. They spent all their time in plant-filled apartments and cafés with excellent wifi. In the long run it was inevitable they would convince themselves that nothing else existed.

The future appeared out of focus. They couldn't imagine it being substantially different to their current life – so smooth and manicured – which itself made it seem rather abstract and unenticing. They had grown up in the shadow of the turbulent sixties and seventies; their grandparents had lived through the war and been tossed about by the raging seas of a century that had now ended, leaving only calm in its wake, as far as the eye could see. They would have liked to have been in their twenties for the summer of '68 or when the Wall fell. Previous generations had had a much easier time working out who they were and what they stood for. The problems back then might have been more urgent, but they also had clearer solutions. Now there were too many choices, with each one leading off on endless branches, preventing any real change. Their idea of a revolutionary future didn't go beyond gender balance on corporate boards, electric cars, vegetarianism. Not only had Anna and Tom not had the chance to fight for a radically different world, but they couldn't even imagine it.

That nostalgia was a little hypocritical. The migration crisis had hovered at the edges of the headlines for years, but they had dismissed it as a Mediterranean problem, and therefore no longer theirs. It didn't concern them in Berlin, or only in the theoretical way injustices committed far away could be said to concern them.

And yet, by the summer of 2015, news reports of sunken boats and inhumane conditions in migrant detention camps on the North African coast were being published on a daily basis. The infographics showed five- or six-digit figures, routes drawn in red through Mauritania and Algeria, Sudan and Libya, and circular icons over Syria and Afghanistan. The images showed dinghies being pitched about in rough seas and packed with dozens, sometimes hundreds of people wearing tattered life jackets with straps flapping in the wind, or no life jacket at all. The reception facilities for those who survived the journey consisted of tent cities or sunbeaten shipping container sites fenced with concertina wire.

Anna and Tom knew that the migrant pushback policies were inhumane, on a par with the atrocities seen on a daily basis along the US-Mexico border. They condemned both, and felt equally compelled to recognize their privilege and to share the public condemnations that would pop up in their timelines. All their friends felt the same way. Anna and Tom had added a sea rescue organization to their list of monthly donations, and signed petitions calling for Europe to do more. But not even this issue offered the clear-cut solutions they craved. Arguments in favour of open borders were counterbalanced by the proven fact that indiscriminately welcoming migrants fomented xenophobia among the people Anna and Tom vaguely referred to – in part out of contempt, and in part conscious of their own privilege – as 'unskilled workers'. They didn't know what to do beyond be outraged by the situation. Over time, the image of migrants crammed into dinghies beside grey military patrol boats became a staple of their information landscape, their eyes processing them in the same way they did the dusty yellow photos of wars in the Middle East, or the red and cobalt blue of the smoke grenades at G8 protests.

All that changed with the images of the drowned boy.

He was lying face down on the shoreline, his arms by his sides. The sea was lapping at his head, the water lead-grey against the dark sand. He was wearing blue shorts and a red T-shirt that rode up to reveal his tummy. From some of the pictures it looked like he was sleeping, but they weren't the ones that circulated the most. In the pictures that circulated the most, you could see the water licking his face, underscoring the unnaturalness of his pose, the absence of any reflex. You could tell from his open fists that his muscles had stiffened. There was one close-up with the soles of his shoes in the foreground, but most of the images had been taken from further away to include a longer stretch of coast in the background. The figure of that lifeless little body was slightly off-centre, and not far from him stood a man wearing a military cap and an official-looking vest, inexplicably in the same red and blue as the boy's clothes. The man, seen from behind, was standing in his boots just beyond the surf's reach, which reflected the livid, petrol-blue sun. He was looking at the drowned boy with a phone in his hand, as if taking a photo. The detachment in his posture was even more strikingly unnatural than that of the corpse at his feet, a tiny discarded thing, no bigger than the washed-up debris around him.

That image had the symbolic power of history-making photographs, and was reproduced with extraordinary speed on social media, in newspapers, on the TV and on illegal posters stuck up at the protests. To Anna and Tom it seemed destined to define their age, like the tank man or the napalm girl. It had been circulating for barely a week when the German government opened its borders to a million Syrian refugees.

Word that a reception centre would be set up on the site of the old Tempelhof airport hit people's timelines like a blaring air-raid siren, and mobilized Anna and Tom's circle in a way that would have been unimaginable only days before. Overnight, the activism on their social media had trickled down to the real city, and Anna and Tom let themselves be carried along by it. They were driven by the urgency of the humanitarian crisis, of course, but also by the feeling that something was taking place around them that they didn't want to miss, an outstanding rendezvous with history.

Their inboxes were suddenly bursting with fundraising appeals, calls to action, invitations to join mailing lists, shared calendars and documents. An anonymous group of volunteers had put together a basic German–Arabic phrasebook in Excel and uploaded it to Google Drive. Anna and Tom offered to typeset it, but someone else got there first: the asymmetric paragraphs were placed in a restrained and legible grid, centre aligned with wide margins and an elegant sans-serif font. An art printer had gone ahead and made a first print run, which others were already handing out at the hotspots.

Anna and Tom offered up their address as a collection point for donations, which would be picked up periodically by someone in a van who would then take them to Tempelhof. The doorbell would ring at all hours, but mostly between 10 a.m. and 1 p.m., when they would be handed tote bags from architecture magazines or blue IKEA bags filled with old fleece blankets, hiking boots, toys and gloves. The donors were always roughly their age, sometimes accompanied by a dog or all-terrain buggy. They were mostly Americans, but also, surprisingly, Germans. Their faces were vaguely familiar from the Portuguese café on Sonnenallee, one of the many illegal DJ sets in Hasenheide or some or other opening. But these encounters struck them as more authentic. The looks they exchanged with the people who showed up at their door, bearing bags of tattered sheepskin jackets and American Apparel organic tees, were charged with a silent recognition of their shared struggle. They were part of a community, citizens of something much bigger than the English-speaking spaceship that had set them down in Berlin.

Anna and Tom would reply to emails, catalogue the donated items and then take them down onto the street themselves to save the volunteer drivers from having to find parking. They would post testimonies and photos from the volunteers on board the NGO ships. Their days would be swallowed up by the constant stream of information reaching them online – there weren't enough tents; the phone chargers kept short-circuiting so they needed more extension cables, but also more nappies, and more cars. Their clients were understanding about the inevitable delay to their deadlines, and even encouraged them. When Anna and Tom wrote to the kombucha brewery in Plänterwald to say that their flyer would be two weeks late, they received an automatic reply explaining that all deliveries were suspended while their van was needed elsewhere.

Many hours were spent discussing what more they could do to help. Together they would assemble in the enormous living rooms of their flat shares in Graefekietz, or in Facebook groups, or in circles of folding chairs in empty gallery spaces, to ask themselves the difficult questions, to ask themselves what role they could play in that epoch-defining moment for their city. By 'they', Anna and Tom understood the graphic designers and digital marketing professionals, the freelance writers, architects, artists and programmers – people with desirable and, in a way, specialist skills who were nonetheless struggling to make any use of them in the present circumstances. Very few had serviceable German, none spoke any Arabic; the NGOs were only looking for people with experience at sea or in rescue missions. By 'they', Anna and Tom did not understand, or at least not explicitly, anyone who could be considered an expat, a term they tended to apply either ironically or judgementally. And yet that term did apply to them, and in the frenzy of their mobilization and the meta-frenzy of their attempt to theorize that mobilization, no one was able to say why that abbreviation applied to some expatriates and not to others.

Every so often Anna and Tom would go down to Tempelhof in person. The tents initially erected on the grass between the runways had now been moved to a hangar in preparation for autumn. They were separated by plastic dividers covered in graffiti and drawings. A constant din filled the air, which smelled of damp clothes and mud. The refugees looked exhausted, distraught, confused. Some were furious about their treatment, but most were overcome with speechless gratitude despite the clear inadequacy of the facilities and the growing suspicion that the present humanitarian effort was essentially motivated by a need for cheap labour. The adults were required to take German-language Integrationskurs to help them enter the workforce, while the children (all but left on their own to process the trauma of their journey and uprooting) would run around the camps in gaggles, shouting and playing in the dirt. Copies of the elegantly typeset phrasebook lay abandoned here and there, their pages rippled and damp from the humidity. Everybody used the translation apps on their phones.

Anna and Tom found it increasingly hard to feel useful. They offered to help look after the children, but they couldn't understand them, and were also, to their shame, a little intimidated. The passport office needed interpreters, but their German wasn't up to it. The volunteer mediators between the police and the refugees would snap when someone asked them to repeat themselves in English.

It was hard to justify their presence there. Whenever a fresh load of donations came in, they would spend the morning fishing through bags for pairs of shoes and socks to hand out to people in line, but the donation scheme was put on hold after a case of bedbugs. In the end they put themselves down for kitchen shifts, where they would spend four hours a week serving bowls of soup. They would get home with headaches and chapped lips from the wind and post a photo of the lunch queue, or call for more volunteers. Warming their hands on a hot mug of genmaicha, they would watch the likes and shares go up and still feel sure they were doing the right thing.

But despite what the pictures suggested, they weren't actually achieving much, and they would be the first to admit it. As time passed, they noticed more and more signs that something else might be going on. A group of housing activists picketed outside the camp every day, claiming it was the first step in a fresh attempt to redevelop Tempelhof. A national newspaper openly mocked a Canadian artist, particularly active in the organizational mailing lists, and her virtual reality film intended to give the German public a better understanding of the tragic migrant experience. Volunteers were now being asked by NGOs not to bring in smartphones or video cameras, because the many filmmakers and video-artists trying to document the camp at Tempelhof had only generated tensions between the refugees and the police.

More and more often, Anna and Tom wondered what they were doing there in the mud, understanding neither the refugees' questions nor the German authorities' directives, their feet frozen numb, their ears ringing, attracting the dirty looks of police and rescue crews alike. Within their circles, uptake to the movement was so unanimous as to appear unforced, but now they wondered if it hadn't been more about themselves. Of course, it helped prove that the ethical impulse they had shown on social media was genuine, and had merely lacked a practical outlet in the real world. They belonged to a specific time and place, and responded to the events around them. But ultimately the only way they could be of any real help was by using their skills; there would be other crises, in the near or not-so-near future, to which they would be better equipped to respond. Their current efforts had been misguided, and probably pointless. Looking around, that was painfully clear to them.

The February snow and gradual removal of the refugees to public housing marked the beginning of their political disengagement. The group emails slowed down. The last evening meeting in the gallery on Hobrechtstraße ended with a pledge to renew their commitment come April, when the sea crossings would ramp up again. But it was postponed until after Gallery Weekend, and then until after the Biennale, and by then it would be summer.

They couldn't say exactly what had changed after the immediate urgency of the migration crisis passed. In many ways, life carried on as normal. They worked. They attended openings. They partied. They could still be captivated by the beauty of the sun shining down on the Fernsehturm, framed by a sloping Hermannstraße, but their inconclusive, largely wasted efforts over the previous months had left them tired and frustrated. They had glimpsed – within themselves and those around them – a flakiness and vanity that they could not now unsee. They were restless.

They would have liked things to go back to how they were before. Either that or they needed a drastic change. It had all become too samey. Something needed to be rethought. But what? They didn't want children, didn't want to move to a new city; inevitably it came down to money.

On Saturdays they would sit down at the double desk where they had spent the week working and make vague plans. They could take on more clients. Open an agency. The promise of a steady, secure income had never been enough to convince them to accept the in-house positions their clients periodically offered them. In their minds, the very idea of office work had something shameful and defeatist about it – although this feeling was far from clearly defined. Whenever they were overstretched by a project, they would outsource help, finding recent Croatian or Italian graduates on social media to come and typeset from their living room for a few weeks. Now the prospect of a real office seemed more appealing. Working from home was convenient, and certainly made life cushier, but they could also see the advantages of a routine, a morning commute on foot. Spending the entire week between the same four walls could be suffocating.

They would talk it over at picnics by the Landwehr-kanal, or in the sauna at Soho House, where some of their well-connected friends were members. Making plans galvanized them. They would come up with Nordic-sounding names for their agency, visualize them in a stencil Helvetica Neue Light font, and then jot them down on a growing list in the notes app on their phones. Sometimes they would check to see if the web domains were available. They would get carried away with the details, imagining the logo, the viral video to attract a client base, the tropical plants they would display in the shop window, made-to-measure tables at Modulor and whether to pour a resin floor or reclaim the natural linoleum under the GDR tiles.

A few years ago it would have been so easy. There were unoccupied spaces everywhere. Now they regretted not having thought of it sooner. Whenever they did chance upon a ZU VERMIETEN sign in a vacant shop window, they would take a photo of the number and try to call. They would even agree to go through with the odd open house as long as it wasn't through an agency. They had viewed a series of tiny rooms on Dieffenbachstraße with tatty wallpaper and wood-panelled corridors, and a former call centre around Kottbusser Tor with a triangular floorplan and vinyl surfaces everywhere. But the rental prices were always too high – not totally unfeasible, but only achievable with sacrifices they weren't prepared to make. They did once put in an offer on a place, but it was rejected because their income didn't offer sufficient guarantee.

They could have rented a desk in a shared office. Recently, many of the galleries and dance studios based in Kreuzberg's yellow-brick industrial buildings had been converted into co-working spaces. The monthly fee included free healthy snacks and great wifi. They already came with house plants. Anna and Tom knew several people who worked in one and had nothing but good things to say about it. It would have made sense to start there and see how the business developed.

But doing things steadily went against everything they knew. They did a thing properly or not at all; a co-working space, far from spelling the start of something, would have been a step backwards from the spacious comfort of the office they had set up at home. It would have been a waste of money.

It always came back to that. Anna and Tom had never felt they didn't earn enough. Since moving to Berlin their incomes had grown year on year; their lifestyle, though, had remained the same. They never struggled to pay the bills, and hadn't had to give up any small luxuries, but over time they had begun to see what they had lose value. All around them, a second hierarchy was emerging that had nothing to do with age or experience. It was no longer a given that a spacious apartment in an Altbau building would be occupied by someone who had arrived at the start of the millennium. The laptops crowding café tables became wider and more matte. Smartphones grew bigger every year. Porsches and Teslas spread south from Kollwitzkiez, where they would squeeze into parking spots between skips filled with building rubble. Original Eames chairs started cropping up in the apartments of friends, next to Hartwig chessboards, Le Corbusier daybeds and Castiglioni floor lamps with perforated marble block bases.

Anna and Tom felt no desire for that kind of ostentation, but it did open their eyes to a world of possibilities closed off to them. Over the years their rates had remained more or less the same. They didn't have much leverage, because local clients preferred to work with Germans and

English-speaking clients would go with native speakers. This topic, like money, was never brought up in conversations with friends.

Since they couldn't earn any more for their work, they would have do more of it. They gave themselves a year to increase their income enough to secure the space they wanted. After putting in a few pitches for jobs they clearly had no interest in, they were finally hired to come up with a new visual concept for a chain of hotels in and around Friedrichshain and Prenzlauer Berg – logo, web presence, brochures, bar and restaurant menus, dishware, linen, loyalty programme. It was a lot of work. It was exactly what they were looking for.

For months all they did was work. They ordered in noodles or falafels from local restaurants and ate them at their computers. They turned down all but a few invitations and were greeted like long-lost castaways when they did treat themselves to a gallery opening, usually on their way to or from a construction site or a meeting at their client's HQ to go over paper stock samples. They went to bed with bloodshot eyes and dreamed they were walking through the woods with the Photoshop toolbars floating in front of them, inviting them to clone-stamp a pine forest or stream. If they spilled some coffee, their first instinct was to press Command-Z. The apartment fell into an unprecedented state of disarray, with pizza boxes, piles of dirty laundry and dust everywhere. Yet Anna and Tom were buzzing. Their exhausted faces in the mirror reflected an image they didn't recognize. Those months of obsessive, monkish focus represented a new kind of adventure. And seeing themselves from the outside, they seemed somehow revitalized. They already sensed that they would look back on that period as a significant time in their lives. At the start of the job they had divided the flat fee by the number of days they had to deliver, and every evening they would write down the day's earnings on a sheet of ruled paper stuck to the side of the fridge. They would switch off their overheating computers, drink a herbal tea and watch the sum steadily grow, like a beloved plant. This time next year they would be furnishing their new agency from a once again immaculate apartment and they would look back with knowing fondness at the feverish period that had made it all possible. They looked forward to that moment even more than to the money.

The client pulled out three months into the six they had originally requested. It wasn't that they were unhappy with Anna and Tom's work – so satisfied were they, in fact, that the board decided they had done enough, and the rest they could carry on in-house. The kill fee was a quarter of the sum they had agreed on. After a couple of tentative meetings with Steglitz-based lawyers who spoke in slow, blunt English, Anna and Tom had agreed to the terms. The amount was marginally more than they would normally have earned in the same timeframe, but during those three months they had hardly spent any money, so overall they made a gain. But all in all it hadn't been worth it. They took the balance sheet down from the fridge and spent two whole days cleaning the house with Netflix blathering on in the background.

It took them a couple of weeks to find new commissions and gear themselves up to work on them. By then, the additional earnings had mostly been spent, and by the end of the year they would barely see any difference in their income. It was better this way – they wouldn't have wanted too stark a reminder of what might have been. Over time, the memory of those energized days soured into a painful chapter in their personal histories, a failed or at least futile transformation.

For a long time, their crises had always been short-lived. Nothing had ever challenged their belief that they had made the right choices, were where they were supposed to be. They only had to look around to allay any creeping doubts: it was clear from all the people who were either treading or had trodden the same path that it was the right one. Those were the people they would see spending long, lazy Sundays spread out on the grass at Tempelhof, or smoking cigarettes outside book readings at Pro qm.

But their network had also begun to disintegrate. Slowly but surely, their circle of friends was shrinking. The artists among them would apply for Quereinsteiger apprenticeships to retrain as interaction designers, user experience architects or SEO ninjas. The luckiest among them might get a lectureship and move to Bochum, Wuppertal or Lindau. Others tested the limits of the job centre's patience and, after the last instalment of Harz IV benefits, used their Spanish or French to get customer service jobs for start-ups. They discovered company health insurance and pension plans, and soon decided to make up for lost time by putting all their energy into their work. They would respond in the evening to Anna's and Tom's messages from that morning suggesting a beer in the sun or a bike ride. Some used their new employment benefits to finally allow themselves the long-delayed child. They still came to the occasional opening, in the very early evening, a non-alcoholic beer in one hand and a three-wheeler buggy in the other. They would promise to invite Anna and Tom for dinner at theirs soon, really soon. They refused to give up their social life for their kids, who all had names like Otto or Ada so that both extended families could pronounce them. But the logistical hurdles almost always got the better of them, and whenever they did manage to meet up, at the ping-pong table at Arkonaplatz, with a load of other new parents, Anna and Tom could sense, in their mutual awkwardness, that their friendship was fading.

In other cases, their friends would simply disappear. The increasingly feverish pace of change in the city was turning against the people who had fuelled it. As they moved closer to their mid-thirties, their friends, even the old-timers, would suddenly decide to move back... but back where? They would use the term 'back home', surprising even themselves that Berlin was not it.

The decision was usually made for them. The life they had been building for years would prove too vulnerable to collapse. An eviction notice would land on their doorstep and the Mieterverein would be powerless against the Eigenbedarf. An unplanned pregnancy would make it impossible to sign up for German health insurance, or would call for a bigger apartment, from which they were now priced out. The subletters would get divorced and drop their lives in Paris or Umeå to return to Berlin, kicking out their long-term Berlin tenants with no warning. There would be queues around the block for open houses, Bavarian families with binders full of payslips, developers with bank statements in dollars and balances inflated by IPOs.

Like an epidemic striking down members of a community, the desertions were only ever discussed uneasily and in passing. Someone would ask after Pasquale or Veronika, and someone else would reply that they had left. The conversations would end there, no questions asked, as if it were a fact of life. Slowly but surely, Anna and Tom found themselves alone.

The same scene that had once welcomed them so

warmly now made them feel like imposters. Their friends' indie art spaces and small galleries either closed down due to rising fair fees, sold out to blue-chip galleries or moved to Brussels, Naples or Leipzig, which had been the new Berlin for over a decade. The new art spaces that replaced them were set up by a younger crowd fresh out of Goldsmiths or Bard. They dressed in menacing Balenciaga and Vetements coats and all seemed to know each other already. Some of those places – like the bar filled with flowers where a single painting would be hung each month, or the tiny theatre that staged pretentious philosophical performances in English – went completely over their heads. The queue at Berghain kept getting longer, or their patience shorter.

They rarely felt like going out anymore on Saturdays. The street markets were inauthentic, overrun by stalls selling copper wire candleholders, tillandsias, scented soap. Without their old network of friends, contemporary art went back to seeming capricious and obscure. They would spend entire meals browsing Netflix's recommendations. They would look for a film they had read about online only to discover it wasn't available in their territory. They would dip into a series but switch it off halfway through the first repetitive, algorithmically produced episode. They would start a promising documentary, then realize they had already seen it. In the end, for lack of alternatives more than anything, they would head out for one of their strolls.

Not even that could lift their mood. Walking their usual routes, they would invariably notice the changes. The old Croatian lady's Spätkauf was now a 'cake boutique' with a teal-blue shop sign and an Instagram handle written on a blackboard. The cultural centre where the old Greeks used to play cards was now the flagship store of a

Japanese trainer brand. Immense shop windows revealed row after row of indistinguishable offices with a faintly hip feel – design or architecture studios, co-working spaces, start-ups, all with Modulor tables and minimalist Helvetica Neue stencils. Walking past the Art Nouveau apartment blocks off Mehringdamm or the futuristic 1960s high-rise tower blocks around Kottbusser Tor, Anna and Tom would note the growing number of windows with the lights off at night, a likely sign that they were short-term rentals, which meant more speculation.

As they walked, the story of their years in Berlin would unfold around them, set far more firmly in the physical space of the city than in their memories. There, on the ground floor of that corner building, was Elvira's apartment, with its screeching roller shutter that they had nicknamed 'the iron curtain'. There, outside that florist, they would sometimes meet the Bosnian guy who dealt them MDMA. There was Enrique and Miguel's old apartment, two floors up from a brothel. The pair had moved to Berlin cash-rich from a redundancy payout, and had intended to stay in the city before the winter chased them away. When was that, like, six years ago now? There was the restaurant where they used to eat poached eggs with Angeliki, who made a living subletting her two-bed apartment to Norwegian art students. They hadn't heard from her in a while, and guessed the Finanzamt had finally caught up with her.

Those memories were sweet but they seemed to belong to another life entirely. For a long time, it was precisely those little details that made them feel at home – the different types of paving on the streets, the citrus motifs on the cornices covered in graffiti, the tropical plants behind the bay windows. Now that feeling had gone, even if the details that had produced it remained the same. It

85

felt uncanny, wrong. And the more they thought about it, the less Anna and Tom could tell whether the change had occurred in the city, so much more open in their twenties, or in them, who were now closer to forty.

Space had ceased to be limitless. In the evenings, Tempelhof would be filled with joggers, the bike lights on their Lycra vests blinking a trail like sonar pulses. The vacant lots had gone, and in their place turnkey apartment complexes had been built – or rather, materialized fully completed. These buildings were remarkably similar in design; they all shared pretensions of exclusivity, with grids of precast concrete beams and pillars creating a checkerboard frame for flat glass panels. They had five or six floors, all with floor-to-ceiling windows, some spanning two storeys, others set back to make room for a small balcony. None of them had curtains, not even on the lower floors, meaning passers-by could look through the glass walls and observe every last detail of the lives going on inside those luminous cubes, with interiors so sleek and so similar to one another it made you wonder if they had been built like that, occupied as standard. They had steel kitchen islands and track shelving units displaying studiously spaced ornaments and vases. The tables would be made of glass or soft-edged wood, the bedframes upholstered in either cream fabric or dark leather. The walls would be hung with abstract paintings and Danish sound systems. Every so often you would glimpse the figure of a man – and it was always a man – standing at the kitchen counter, dressed in dark clothes and slowly sipping from a wine glass. They moved with an almost unreal slowness. They seemed trapped in a pocket of light in the darkness of the city, as if in a fish tank.

But if Anna and Tom watched them for too long the perspective would reverse, and suddenly they would be overcome, dizzied, by the feeling that it was they who were trapped.

REMOTE

They tried travelling.

The trips paid for themselves. Their apartment would be fully booked without fail within hours of them listing it, thanks to those simple, pristine photos, so carefully curated. They spent a few long weekends by the Baltic Sea, the odd off-season week in the Alps or on Greek islands – places with wide, uninterrupted views and good wifi. They would decide the dates and then plan their trip as soon as they received a booking for their apartment, their excitement building almost to a frenzy. They would scroll through the photos of their destinations, falling in love, then study the different hikes and plan where to eat. They had a clear mental image of what they were looking for: leisurely, light-filled days spent in nature, with space for five or six hours of work on their laptops, curled up on the sofa looking out at a great expanse of sky over some barren beach on the Ostsee coast. Or early evenings spent lazily answering emails and drinking wine and sparkling water from a whitewashed clifftop terrace.

Not only was all of this possible, it would be surprisingly easy: the earnings to be made on tourist rentals in Berlin would cover the cost of their flights and more. Life was so simple. Tiny bowls of olives, tiny plates of Matjessalat. The taste of salt on their skin. They had so much freedom at their fingertips, limitless opportunity to explore. They were amazed they hadn't thought of it sooner.

The immediate effects of that freedom were less clear-cut. Somehow, between airport transfers and unforeseen events, their initial budget always proved optimistic. Their time management also left something to be desired. Getting ready to leave always seemed to take up the entire day before they were due to travel; work left over from the week meant they had little time to enjoy the weekends; off-season weather proved unreliable, as did the restaurant reviews, and the wifi. More often than not they returned to Berlin tired and behind on deadlines. They came home to new scuffs on the walls and ate the guests' leftover food rather than getting a takeaway, to compensate for the taxi from Tegel. They put off doing the laundry until the next day, and then the next, until the weekend.

But each time, after a while, they would remember those trips more generously, as if the act of remembering could alter the experience itself. Scrolling through their profiles, they would pause at the old photos of their laptops on makeshift tables on a beach, aperitif glasses glinting in the sun while in Berlin it dumped with snow, and the seductiveness of the images made them forget all the stress that lay just out of frame. The life depicted in those photos was free and exciting. They were also the photos with the most likes, and the ones that tended to attract comments months after being posted. It had to be a sign of something, to mean something. Invariably they would come to the conclusion that they should give it another go. They had been stupid not to appreciate those experiences in the moment. It seemed so obvious with hindsight.

Those short getaways got them thinking about a more radical change. For work purposes, they needed to be in a big city, but they could consider a career change, learn how to do something more authentic. They imagined themselves as vets, driving in a jeep along forested tracks with a dog in the passenger seat, heading to some remote stables. Or else in a converted barn, now a white-tiled workshop, packing artisanal cheeses flecked with herbs and spices in waxed paper, the air smelling of rennet and hay. Of course these were just fantasies. They knew that if one day they did move, it would be to carry on working at their laptops. But it was those daydreams in the first place that helped them formulate that 'if'. Once that internal shift happened, the rest was a matter of logistics and luck.

In the summer of 2017 they chanced upon a story posted by the same hotel chain that had hired them for the rebrand the year before. The video showed a tall, narrow building with a gleaming blue and gold facade, wrought-iron French balconies and a turret on the roof. The setting wasn't immediately obvious, but it was clear it wasn't Berlin. The camera made its way through a hallway with creaking original floorboards, then led the viewer up a narrow spiral staircase and out onto a roof terrace with a view of the glittering green ocean. *Our new home, your new home*, the overlay read. A caption explained how a group of digital entrepreneurs had bought an old guesthouse in Lisbon's historic centre and were looking for creatives to help reimagine the aesthetic while preserving the spirit of... Anna and Tom clicked 'reply' before they had even finished reading. They were hired.

It would be a fixed-term, part-time arrangement, at a reduced fee but including two months' accommodation in one of the suites inside the hotel itself, which was still being renovated. It seemed too good to be true: they would literally be paid to be on holiday, and in the city that many were saying was becoming the new Berlin – only with Mediterranean food, mild winters and the sea. They could even consider moving there, starting over with a lower cost of living, albeit higher than it was barely a year ago. But even in their delight at this new transformation, they felt a hint of disappointment for not having thought of it sooner. That feeling soon passed.

It wasn't goodbye to Berlin, but it was nonetheless a parting. They would only be put up in the hotel during October and November, but they decided to leave their next move to fate, subletting their apartment for a whole six months. If they were enjoying themselves, they would stay in Lisbon. Otherwise they would see out winter on an island somewhere in Greece or Italy being digital nomads (an expression that never failed to irritate them, but even they could sense the envy beneath their contempt). They cleared out their apartment even more thoroughly than usual, and packed second suitcases with more clothes to leave in a neighbour's loft. This time they found tenants without the letting platform – a couple, both interaction designers newly arrived from Portland and willing to spend their company relocation package on a rent so expensive Anna and Tom felt almost guilty accepting it. The two women were delighted to have all those plants to take care of and promised to look the couple up when they visited Lisbon for the Web Summit.

They also went to Anna and Tom's leaving party, bringing a tray of organic samosas and a vape loaded with CBD. Anna and Tom, surrounded by friends, with their bags packed and an exciting new city awaiting them, their apartment dotted with candles and an autumn rainstorm pounding at the windows, soaked up a feeling of freedom and adventure that they hadn't felt for a long time. They took a load of photos, the light soft and warm, pupils dilated, faces ruddy from the first cold days, but none of those pictures managed to fully capture that feeling, which they both feared losing the moment they left – an illogical fear, given it was precisely because they were leaving that they were feeling it.

In Lisbon, summer was still in the air. A taxi drove them

down winding lanes too narrow for the trams, with pavements dotted with chairs and tables, the cobbles loose here and there from the roots of blue jacarandas. The late-September evening light reflected off the tiled facades, the windows, the windscreens of cars and the slivers of ocean visible between the buildings – the effect was of the sun shining in all directions at once. The hotel was in Bairro Alto, up a tiny backstreet that the taxi driver refused to enter for fear she'd scratch her car. An unmarked door opened onto a small square courtyard with glass walls on three sides and three metal tables competing for the shade of a palm tree. Closing their eyes, Anna and Tom breathed in the smell of sea salt and eucalyptus bark picked up on the wind, and imagined they were in South America. But when they opened them again they saw the brushed concrete flooring, the rubber plant, the bar with its Danish redesign, and it felt like they were in Berlin. The spiral staircase from the video led to the rooms on the first floor and then to a terrace above, with commanding views over the whole city. From there you could see the ocean, the churches, the umbrella pine groves, the grand seafront avenues and the clusters of crumbling tenements in the centre, and it felt like they were in languorous southern Europe, which, of course, they were.

Their room, which was not a suite, was awaiting renovation. The walls were a dusty beige, with brown streaks in several places; the veneer on much of the furniture was chipped or peeling, revealing the moisture-damaged chipboard underneath. The room was spacious enough, but it contained no less than four single beds, two of which had been pushed together, meaning Anna and Tom struggled to squeeze their cases between that makeshift double and the wardrobe. The bed bases immediately strained under their weight, with a creak of old springs and a whiff of mustiness from the mattress. The room's sole window overlooked the internal courtyard, which was in total shade. The bathroom had no window at all.

Anna and Tom agreed to ask to be moved, but said no more about it. They were excited for the start of their adventure and didn't want to kill the mood. They would be meeting their clients the following day for breakfast, but for now decided to go out and find a nice spot to watch the sun go down with a beer. They each chose one of the spare beds to use as a wardrobe, then quickly changed and left. In an effort to downplay that somewhat squalid first impression, they told themselves they would spend most of the next two months working from the main lobby, or exploring the city. This, at least, was the plan.

That first evening they took a long walk through the winding streets of the old town, climbing in search of a view. They drank a couple of beers while watching a partial sunset from the Santa Catarina lookout. The sun sank behind the horizon with a speed and intensity of red that didn't exist in Germany. The breeze picked up and felt cool, but not unpleasantly so. They overheard English, Portuguese and French being spoken around them, and the couples and groups of twenty-somethings looked so like the ones they remembered from their early days in Berlin it almost felt like they had gone back in time. They could picture themselves living there, for the simple reason that they had once already. They ordered bacalhau à Brás at a tiny restaurant based in an apartment, and got lost twice before finally making it back to the hotel, feeling weighed down by dinner and their metamorphosis.

They established a routine surprisingly fast. The work was repetitive and easy – all they had to do was add a Mediterranean twist and a taste of Lisbon to the style guides they themselves had come up with for the Berlin hotels. They took a co-working space in the lobby. Whenever the sound of jigsaws and hammers got too much, they would go out and explore the city, supposedly to get mood board inspiration, but really hoping to recover the wanderlust that had defined their early days in Berlin.

And there was something about Lisbon that struck them as similar. The crumbling Art Nouveau apartment buildings had plants in every window, or had undergone more fishtank renovations with new extensions in glass and steel; the blackboards in front of the cafés advertised pastéis instead of Nordsee-Frühstück, but the brand of oat milk in their flat whites was the same. The aluminium laptops glinting on outdoor tables were also the same, but the beer labels said Sagres not Tannenzäpfle, and the wifi was shakier. The galleries and indie art spaces were also there – Helvetica stencils on the windows and reclaimed wooden floors creating a nice contrast with the cold white walls – even if the art wasn't as conspicuously hip. The little tourist shops sold typical tiles instead of pieces of wall. It was all different, which was what they had wanted; and yet it was also somehow all the same. They had wanted that too, but still they weren't satisfied. In Lisbon, Anna and Tom were bored.

Within a few days they had run out of ideas for what to do with their time. The beach was cold if you weren't a surfer. Without their usual circle of friends, they weren't bothered about seeing exhibitions. The city was so charming, so rich with history that their explorations of it felt samey and touristy, which wasn't how they liked to see themselves. With nothing else going on around it, their work felt tedious. Eating out was cheaper than in Berlin, but there was also less variety. All the films there were dubbed and incomprehensible, and in any case the mere idea of going to the cinema felt like admitting defeat. They had rediscovered the abundance of time, but somehow it felt like time wasted. Enthusiasm eluded them, always just out of reach.

They took long walks up and down the stepped streets around Bairro Alto, Castelo and Graça. They gazed at the window displays of grand old-fashioned food stores in the lower city. It dawned on them how impractical and expensive it was to live for longer than a few days in a kitchenless hotel room. They met some new people – an Italian gallerist, a French astrologer, a handful of coders and journalists who had passed through Berlin some years back and then landed up there in Lisbon – but those encounters never developed into friendships. They would exchange a bit of banter across benches at a mira-douro, or ask them for a charger or a bottle opener, but the conversation never developed beyond exchanging pleasantries and details of how long they had been in the city – two months, two years, on a temporary basis but open to staying, depending on the situation with housing, on their jobs, on the weather. They sized each other up based on where they sat on the scale between tourist and expat. When they searched on Facebook for mutual friends, they either didn't share any or they were people they didn't really know.

The truth was, Anna and Tom would have liked to befriend these people, meet up again to go out for dinner or partying or to an opening, but they felt a bit desperate proposing it. They didn't want to come across as clingy, or needy. How had they done it in the early days in Germany? This wasn't so different. But something about their age then, and the sense of being part of a movement, had made it so much easier to make plans with strangers, taking it as given that they would become friends. Now, walking back to the hotel after an evening out, they would talk about how Tiago was nice, Azzurra was clearly on coke, James looked like someone they used to see out and about in Neukölln. But they didn't delude themselves that those acquaintances would develop into friendships, which they weren't even convinced they wanted. So what did they want?

Increasingly they spent their evenings at the same bar near the Jardim de São Pedro de Alcântara, drinking ice-cold Sagres and browsing social media to see what was happening in Berlin.

As autumn progressed, a hushed excitement started to build in the cafés and squares where the expats hung out. Conversations overheard in English became more frequent and louder. The Web Summit was about to take place, attracting people from all over the world, which in practice meant from the east and west coasts of the US, Berlin and London. The hotel's official opening would coincide with the first day of the summit, but it started accepting guests a couple of days before.

One by one they arrived, pulling suitcases big enough to last them the duration of the special *digital nomads* package (Anna and Tom knew it well, having designed the promotional materials): five, ten or twenty weeks at half board, with added extras like taxi vouchers, a series of organized aperitifs, flash talks and mindfulness courses.

On the first day of the summit the hotel threw a party for their new guests and the new website went live, marking the end of their contract. Anna and Tom had planned to stay on for a few weeks, only to be told that the hotel was fully booked after the summit. They told themselves that this was a good thing, as it would spur them to find somewhere more homely. That night they hung out until late in the hotel courtyard, which was packed with block-chain analysts and teenage entrepreneurs practising the pitches they would make over the following days to angel investors on anyone drunk enough to listen. The party was sponsored by a vodka brand and very soon everyone was drunk. They met someone there who knew their Berlin subtenants, who had actually written to Anna and Tom to say they were on their way to Lisbon, but then went quiet. They accepted a dab of ketamine. At one point they found themselves in a taxi with a taciturn Irish hacker and a young Israeli woman with pink hair droning on about the future of AI. They were heading to an event the woman had heard about on Twitter and to which a famous billionaire with ambitions to resettle humankind on Mars had apparently showed up, but at some point the woman decided the photo was photoshopped, a promotional hoax, and redirected the driver towards a house party.

They got out in front of an imposing oceanfront apartment building. The main door was open and even the communal entrance hall was heaving. Everyone looked slightly younger than Anna and Tom, or much younger. They were dressed either in suits with mismatching piercings and neck tattoos, or shiny sportswear. The Israeli woman elbowed her way up two flights of the marble staircase, explaining – in response to their puzzled faces – that the top floor belonged to a psychedelics evangelist who for years had been dealing microdoses for cryptocurrency and had got rich during the first Bitcoin price surge. The music grew louder with every step, but it sounded more like a kind of distant rumbling in that crowded, cavernous space. On the top floor landing the throng was even more tightly packed and the double door was being blocked by two bouncers and a house plant. Beyond it, strobe lighting created a flashing forest of heads; the ceilings were high with faded green period mouldings. One guy was sporting a fluorescent mohawk. Another was crying.

Their two companions exchanged a few shouted words with the bouncers in Portuguese over the EDM, and then quickly slipped into the apartment with an apologetic glance back. Anna and Tom made a half-hearted attempt to get past the bouncers, insisting they look up their names on their tablet guest list in the vague hope that they wouldn't bother and instead would just let them in. But when that failed they didn't insist. Behind them, someone was complaining. They could feel a dull throbbing behind their eyes and in their temples as the ketamine wore off. The atmosphere was stuffy, the flashing oppressive. They hurried down the stairs, sandwiched between the handrail and the queue of people waiting to get in, feeling increasingly in need of some fresh air. Once outside, they sat on the stoop of a shuttered storefront, opened their navigation app and discovered, to their great relief, that they were just a few flights of steps from the hotel.

It took them a long time to fall asleep, under two layers of scratchy blankets. There was no heating in the room, and the single-glazed windows rattled in their frames as sheets of ocean wind gusted against them. The nights were turning cold.

Up until that moment they had both imagined, without fully admitting it, that a reason would come up to spend the remaining four months – and perhaps longer – there in Lisbon; that they would find a cheap, comfortable apartment, a new community, the transformation and growth that Berlin had promised and failed to deliver. Lisbon failed too. After four days of the Web Summit and two months of eating in mediocre restaurants, Anna and Tom needed a proper break, a cosy hideaway to fall back in love with their lives. All the short-term rentals were either booked or too expensive, and – they suspected – probably didn't have heating. They considered splurging a chunk of their savings on a month in what looked from the photos to be a spacious, minimal apartment, but were put off when they realized how similar it was to their place in Berlin.

Several of their friends were planning to spend the following summer in Sicily, and they told themselves it wouldn't be a bad idea to get ahead of the international arts crowd, find themselves a bolthole with a sea view, or a hideaway in the hills to host people en route to Manifesta and work lazily on their projects from a sun-drenched terrace. Of course, they wouldn't be able to find such a place at short notice, from Portugal. Airbnb offered very few options: either tacky, overpriced tourist traps with nauseating inspirational quotes on the walls, IKEA cube shelving and pull-out sofa beds, or dark, dusty apartments crammed with what could only be a dead relative's furniture. Very few had a sea view. Anna and Tom felt encouraged by this, taking it as a sign that the area's potential was still largely untapped. If they asked around, talked to some newsagents and oldies in the local bars, they might just find somewhere with a difference – one that hadn't yet been spoiled by the internet. Anna and

Tom made the very sensible decision to rent a car and a cheap base somewhere inland from which to search for something better.

They would spend their mornings working at a table in the garden and in the afternoons explore the hills that rolled down to the coast. They would end up in a small, forgotten town where dry-stone houses would sell for a euro, paving the way for an influx of creatives from all over Europe. Or they would find a remote fishing village still hostile to tourists and pay a pittance for a small-town lawyer's top-floor apartment in an ugly seafront condominium, complete with a huge terrace framed by reinforced concrete pillars and paved with square pebble slabs.

For the time being they settled for a semi-detached house on the outskirts of Noto with a garden and wifi. From the photos they saw it had a partial view of the hills. The house itself looked ugly – a basic cube with exposed brickwork on the outside and inside yellowing lace curtains and off-white tiles – and was directly attached to the owner's place, but it was very cheap, and the temperatures for December were forecast to be twenty degrees higher than in Berlin. It would do. No, they corrected themselves: it would more than do.

They flew, then drove. The sensation of winding their way through the Mediterranean hills with their bags piled up on the back seat immediately made them feel like they were on an adventure; but the landscape gradually lost its splendour the further they drove from the coast, until it looked like any old countryside, which was what it was. The house was at the far end of a long, dusty drive surrounded by similar-looking houses, which hadn't been visible in the photos. A dog started barking the moment they turned off the engine and didn't stop for several minutes. Once inside – the keys had been left under the doormat – they were greeted by a musty, mouldy smell. Rows of dead flies stood guard at every windowsill, as light and brittle as pressed flowers. Opening the windows just a crack let in the roar of trucks from the Syracuse-Gela motorway on the other side of the hill.

Determined to keep their spirits high, they drank a whole bottle of Cerasuolo in the small dirt patch of a garden while the house aired out. They had only paid for fifteen days, with the possibility of extending their stay if they didn't find anywhere else. They laughed off their bad luck and told themselves they would be out of there before the two weeks were up, even if it meant losing money. Instead, they stayed for four months, the unhappiest of their relationship.

At first they tried their hardest to remain optimistic. They began each day with a stroll through the dusty vineyards, looking for spots where the sound of the traffic was less deafening. Working without an external monitor was uncomfortable, and the wifi had to be rebooted every half-hour, but nonetheless they found a rhythm and were able to concentrate quite well. For lunch they would eat bread, fruit and cheese, then jump into their Nissan Micra rental and set off exploring.

And yet, for whatever reason, they never seemed to find what they were looking for. The dry-stone villages tucked in between hills and the sleepy Sicilian Baroque towns were charming but hostile, closed to them. They struggled to picture themselves there for any real length of time. They spoke to a few estate agents, but no one would rent them an apartment for the duration they needed – longer than short-term, shorter than long-term – and what little there was on the market didn't appeal. These drives often included breathtaking views of rolling vineyards and ochre and ivory church bell towers silhou-etted against a milky blue sky; a fresh sea breeze would rush in through the half-opened windows, drowning out the sound of the electronic music coming from their Bluetooth speaker. There were moments when it felt like they were on holiday or travelling (they weren't), and when they focused on certain details they could sense the possibility of being excited by life again, a little like the feeling of sleep emerging through the darkness of insomnia. Happiness was there, tantalisingly close, and achievable with a simple operation of the mind. But sec-onds later the sight of the concrete shell of a half-finished building, or a dilapidated shopping centre surrounded by rubbish and burned-out cars was enough to remind them they were still very far from what they wanted.

After an hour at the wheel and two spent traipsing up and down identical streets – slippery cobbles, dark ground-floor apartments, overpriced minimarkets, mod-ern buildings with peeling plaster, cars parked on the pavements or at the foot of some church steps – they would stop at a bar to drink a Campari at a plastic table, reminding themselves that they were in Sicily, they were near the sea, they were branching out. In the low sea-son most of the restaurants were closed, so they usually ate at the formica tables of some standard-fare trattoria with glaring neon lights and no vegetarian options. They would leave feeling stuffed on carbs and suspecting they had been ripped off. And the next day they would start all over again.

There was still the coast, of course, but somehow even that was different to how they had pictured it. The fish-ing villages had no fishermen in them, and the little bars around the main piazza weren't patronized by old people playing cards, but by groups of teenagers with ripped bodies and blaring mopeds, who would glare at Anna and Tom in a way that hardly encouraged them to pull out their shiny aluminium laptops. The restaurants all had laminated menus with photos of the dishes and chintzy sailing knots on the walls. There were the stunning views over the horizon at sunset and the small courtyards with potted lemon trees and ivy growing up the dry-stone walls, but they had already all been co-opted by the boutique hotels with SUVs parked out front. What they were looking for must have existed once upon a time, back when you only had to hop onto a train or a ferry to reach a whole other world, an authentic, uncrowded world of dark red house wine in carafes and quiet hideaways by the sea. But now they knew those days were over and that, whether due to a lack of foresight on their part or because they had simply been born a generation too late, they couldn't afford that world today.

They started to bicker. Tom clearly remembered having suggested Greece in the first place. To him, Sicily had always seemed like a bad idea, yet another hyped-up fad among the Berlin scene, who all had their eye on the art Biennale happening the following year. Tom argued that Sicily had been a conformist, lazy choice, in a tone that suggested that the conformist wasn't him. Anna, feeling hurt, remembered all the reasons she had given for them to stay in Lisbon, where they would have had far more to do than just drive around the countryside chasing a dream. The idea of a rural getaway had been all Tom's idea, and they needn't have spent all that time and money to see it was pathetically naive. The end of December brought two weeks of solid rain, which they spent cooped up inside the house, sleeping badly and waking up with sore heads – part migraine, part smouldering resentment. The lights in the house were yellowish and dim, such that it felt like perpetual dusk. They worked in separate rooms, only talking when it was to comment on a layout and graphic on Slack. Work was draining and repetitive. Their first drink of the evening crept forward from seven to six-thirty, then six.

They spent an unmemorable New Year's Eve on a hotel terrace in Catania, watching the fireworks over the sea but with their minds on the hire car down the street, worrying it would get vandalized. They were already drunk by the countdown, and had to force down the bottle of prosecco they popped open on the stroke of midnight. They didn't want to waste it. At twenty to one they went back to their room and had bad sex, which was better than no sex.

In the spirit of New Year's they resolved to make the best of their situation. Their afternoon excursions resumed – they were paying for the car, after all – but they stopped deluding themselves that they were anything other than tourists. They visited baroque churches, limestone villages, wineries perched in the hills between Vittoria and Donnafugata; boggy, blustery nature reserves with that desaturated beauty of the Mediterranean in winter. They treated themselves to a weekend in a high-end hotel set in a converted tuna fishery and overlooking an emerald green cove. They climbed Etna, feeling the searing heat from the lava on their faces, blinded by the glare that hit them from every direction, counting the greenhouses and abandoned housing blocks dotted inland as far as the eye could see. They planned a trip to Levanzo, but had to cancel due to bad sea conditions.

Through all of this they continued to document their remote working life on social media. The pictures were always stunning, enticing – prickly pear groves, Camparis on red plastic beach tables, sunsets over vineyards, carved tufa limestone facades, stray cats, their laptops usually somewhere in the frame to prove they weren't on holiday – evidence of a life of freedom and adventure, one full of beauty and hard work, and with occasional surprises. Yet something in their spirits had changed. Back in the day, looking at images like those and knowing how frustrated and unhappy they had been when they took them made them feel ashamed, deficient, as if the reality presented in the photos should somehow be capable of triumphing over how they really felt, and that their inability to enjoy such a desirable life revealed a flaw in their character. They had outgrown this insecurity. Now those images just seemed like a con.

They watched the likes and the envious comments from friends asking when they could join accumulate with a growing sense of imposture. Once in a while those conversations would develop over text and their friends would send screenshots of flight times and requests for tips about where to stay. But the plans never went anywhere, and it was no surprise to Anna and Tom that they didn't receive a single visitor during the months they were there.

Towards the end of February their subtenants sent them a scan of a threatening letter from the Finanzamt. Anna and Tom could have responded to the letter from Sicily, but instead they used their distrust in the Italian postal service as an excuse to go home early. In Berlin they arrived to snow and a pile of unpaid bills. They had to arrange a bizarre tour of their own apartment, overseen by their tenants, to grab some more winter clothes, which originally they had hoped they wouldn't need. They spent the next three weeks cat-sitting for a friend of a friend in Wedding, resentfully living out of bags like tourists in what was still their city.

When at last they could get back into their apartment, they didn't feel newly returned from a great trip but tired, behind on work and with a load of cleaning to do. Like everyone else, and as in every April in Berlin, they got their heads down and waited for spring. That year it was late.

FUTURE

Spring will come. They will try to settle back into their old life. They will mark the arrival of the warm weather by moving their office to the outdoor tables that the cafés will have pulled out of storage. They will find new clients among the impresarios keen to capitalize on the latest wave of fish smokeries, sourdough bread and poké. They will hazard a few nights out, and find their bodies are less efficient at metabolizing the drugs. With a touch of resentment, they will eye up the state-of-the-art electric road bikes belonging to the new kids from Seattle, Dublin and Frankfurt. They will look at a few jobs posts for in-house positions but lose interest on seeing the requirement for good German or native English. In their downtime they will scroll through the profiles of old schoolfriends, looking for proof that they aren't doing better than them. They will sit around with their old Berlin friends discussing how hard it is now – there, in the city of abundance – to find an apartment, a spot at preschool, a table at the new Indian, an English-speaking therapist, an available charge point for the Tesla.

They will find themselves less and less interested by their job and will spend their days sliding a smart guide one millimetre this way or that, tweaking colours for different interfaces, producing yet another variation on the current look in vogue in their neighbourhood, which could just as well have been New York – or anywhere in the world, for that matter. The static full-screen image with a scrolling textbox overlay. The oversize claim in serif font with a full stop after it. The hamburger menu top left, top right. The sequence of mini video clips as a backdrop. The tablet version. What did they ever see in all that? They will find themselves wondering how long it would be before a neural network could carry out most of their work. They will find themselves wondering whether that would be such a shame. How could they ever have chosen to spend their days like that, hunched over a computer screen in their living room?

But then, had they really chosen it? The reason they had tolerated, even loved the work, they will tell themselves, is because the repetitiveness provided a counterbalance to the limitless growth and broad horizons of the rest of their days. Now, they will realize, nothing remains but the work.

They will catch themselves reminiscing with unreasonable fondness about those miserable few months in Sicily, about the romantic nights spent trembling under two blankets in Lisbon, about the sea breeze roaring through their car in Noto, with the Mediterranean a mere twenty minutes away – although in reality it had been more like an hour. They will be tempted to search elsewhere for what they found all those years ago in Berlin and then tried and failed to find again that winter. But it will prove impossible because that abundance was the result of a specific overlap between the city's history and theirs. Intensely disorientated, they will find themselves unable to disentangle one from the other; and this, their sudden inability to access a version of their past unfiltered by nostalgia, will be their understanding of nostalgia.

How long will they be able go on like this? In theory, forever.

Luck – but it will not be luck exactly – will be on their side. At the end of the summer, Anna's uncle – a childless, single engineer with a passion for extreme sports – will pass away, leaving her the farmhouse that he used his entire life's savings to renovate, imagining for himself a retirement of winemaking and kitesurfing. The house will be located in a coastal region known for hosting lavish weddings for sheiks. Anna and Tom will go down for the funeral at the start of the German autumn and spend two nights there, but within five minutes they will know.

The estate will consist of a farmhouse, barn and granary, plus a scattering of small outbuildings tucked in among the olive groves in the arid, Sirocco-swept hills. The yellowing limestone will be embroidered with creepers; the land will be enclosed by a dry-stone wall that runs alongside the dirt road leading down to the coast. The air will smell of heat, dust, wild fennel and salt; the arid, mineral soil will lend a sharpness to the wine and oil produced there. Anna's uncle had imagined great bonfires with his friends over the endless summers of retirement, independent, spacious rooms for them all, barbecues under the pergola, vintage motorbikes in the barn and the other outbuildings for the wine vats, his kitesurfing equipment and the dinghy. Of course, there will be no reason those friends cannot instead be paying guests.

This parting will be different. First they will arrange a series of meet-ups with their friends to tell them all about their latest venture. They will keep the apartment in Berlin under their names – a rental agreement at that price will be one worth holding onto – but they will find long-term subtenants and leave it to them all but empty. A removal van will set off ahead of them, loaded up with the plants, most of the furniture, the floor-standing speakers, the enamel dishes, the Berber rug, the herringbone blanket, the LPs and most of the glasses, meaning that for their leaving party they will have to pick up some paper cups from the all-hours Späti on Pflügerstraße. They will show their friends photos of the house, the surrounding landscape, the sea just a stone's throw away, and they will sense in the tone of their friends' promises to come and visit that they actually mean it, unlike with Sicily. They will take what they will claim will be their last ever MDMA, really believing it.

Then they will finally leave, excited and emotional, sad to be closing one chapter of their lives but eager to start another. They will take a photo of themselves in the glass doors of Schönefeld's departures terminal, trying to replicate their pose and expressions from all those years before. During the flight they will hold their smartphones up to study the two photos side by side, zooming in to look at the wrinkles and shadows on their faces, and finding there the years passed: two kids leaving, two adults returning.

Winter will be a whirlwind of activity. They will hold onto a few of their existing design contracts, but the work on the house will end up demanding much more than the half-days they had accounted for. They will design all the furniture themselves – pistachio lacquered metal frames, premium three-ply wood, marble tops – and have a local craftsman build it. They will hang oversized exposed lightbulbs around the place, running the cables through copper pipes. They will choose raw bedlinen from Ostwestfalen and enamel bowls. They will find a local young chef happy to think up a simple, authentic breakfast menu. With a limited budget and a lot of emails, they will buy multiples by emerging artists from their friends' galleries, which, together with the furniture, will give their Mediterranean retreat a touch of Berlin edginess. They will pick out cast-iron wood burners and more plants – banyan and rubber trees that they will be able to plant outdoors, there where the climate is more favourable, and also carobs, a small poplar grove and lemon trees.

They will keep part of the upper floor for themselves

112

– a big bedroom, two smaller rooms temporarily serving as offices, a living-room with an ornamental fireplace – and divide the rest of the farmhouse into four bedrooms, two studios with kitchenettes, and a self-contained apartment in the stables. The ground floor will have enough space for a communal living area, library and kitchen.

Then there will be the website, branding and social media presence to consider. It will be the first time they work together like this on a project – not just as designers but also as clients – and for a few weeks they will rediscover their love of graphic design and the joy of drawing that they thought they had lost. They will lay out sample sheets and tableware on the floor to come up with their design scheme, and spend many a happy hour walking among dishes with test designs hand-drawn on them in marker pen. They will document the whole process on Instagram, posting stories about the house renovations and polls to decide the names of the suites (ultimately going with an astrological theme) or to settle a disagreement over the best colour for the menus. They will gain a lot of followers very quickly – some drawn to the beauty of it all, others strategically bought.

They will set themselves a budget for targeted advertising and upper and lower limits for smart pricing. They will bring in a photographer friend who specializes in museum exhibitions, promising her a complimentary three-night stay so that she can photograph the interiors in a series of symmetrical images that have the abstract beauty of renderings. To accommodate any less refined tastes, they will throw in some blander shots: a breakfast table laid with sourdough knäckebröd and jam in the garden; a glass of orange wine reflecting a dry-stone wall and a sunset; a reading nook in the library, flames licking in the fireplace, the armchair enveloped in the cloud-like monstera that will have followed them halfway across the continent.

And just like that, they will open. In May 2019 they will welcome their first intake of guests: from their Berlin circles, two Neapolitan gallerists, a US travel writer and his husband, and a Swedish poet with his latest lover; plus three influencers and two small-town reporters sourced by a local PR agency they will have hired. On arrival, each will find a bottle of local wine, a selection of organic snacks and a handwritten welcome note in their room. The weather will be perfect – sunshine, a sea breeze, evenings just cool enough to appreciate the warm days. The nights will be filled with the song of the cicadas and the smell of wild fennel growing in the cracks of the dry-stone walls.

For Anna and Tom it will be an exhausting weekend. When the last guest leaves on Sunday evening, they will be so worn out they won't even be able to get through the bottle of Franciacorta they will have chilled for the occasion. When they wake up the following day, they will find everything filthy, the rooms turned upside down, and they will spend an entire day tidying up, covered in sweat and dust, listening not to Eurovision songs but to the rattle of the industrial washing machine. They will make an inventory of the traces of wine, coffee and other liquids on the linen sheets. They will spot scratches on the terracotta and cracks in the glasses. They will make time to take some photos for Instagram, but will struggle to crack a smile as they think about all the work still to be done. They will drop barbed remarks about the weekend's hitches, without proposing any solutions. They will drink at lunchtime, doze off in the sun and wake up feeling foggy and sluggish, with a pounding head and too much to do.

But then they will receive notifications of the first reviews, and all that weight will instantly lift. Three will have come in, all of them giving five stars. One will be by a woman with over three hundred thousand followers, who will have tagged them in a post praising, as per their agreement, the relaxed but impeccable welcome, the choice of natural wines, the simple, elegant decor – Mediterranean and yet unmistakably international.

It's all completely perfect, the story will say. *It's just like it is in the pictures.*

Acknowledgements

This novel came about as a tribute to *Things: A Story of the Sixties*, by Georges Perec; anything good in it owes a lot to him. I was able to start it thanks to the hospitality of the Santa Maddalena Foundation, in Donnini, and I finished it with the help of a grant for writers from the Berlin Senate. Though the book is very short, the list of those who helped bring it into existence – with their care, their patience and their work – is long. I am grateful to Natalia Latronico, always; to Morgan Arenson, Davide Coppo, Nicoletta Dalfino, Claudia Durastanti, Irene Fantappiè, Nicola Frau, Stefan Heidenreich, Gideon Lewis-Kraus, Alma Lindborg, Dan Lucas, Tommaso Melilli, Lauren Oyler, Silvia Pelizzari, Veronica Raimo, Marco Rossari, Clara Rubin, Andrea Scarabelli, Clara Miranda Scherffig, Elvia Wilk; to Beatrice von Rezzori, Claire Sabatié-Garat, Marco Vigevani; and to Sophie Hughes, who wrote this book as much as I did.

Donnini, February 2020 – Berlin, June 2021

This book has been translated thanks to a translation grant awarded by the Italian Ministry of Foreign Affairs and International Cooperation.

Questo libro è stato tradotto grazie a un contributo alla traduzione assegnato dal Ministero degli Affari Esteri e della Cooperazione Internazionale italiano.

The authorised representative in the EEA is
eucomply OÜ, Pärnu mnt 139b-14, 11317 Tallinn, Estonia.
hello@eucompliancepartner.com
+33757690241

Fitzcarraldo Editions
133 Rye Lane
London, SE15 4ST
Great Britain

ISBN 978-1-80427-104-9

Design by Ray O'Meara
Typeset in Fitzcarraldo
Printed and bound by Pureprint

fitzcarraldoeditions.com

Fitzcarraldo Editions